#13

JUNIOR HIGH

WHO'S HAUNTING THE EIGHTH GRADE?

JUNIOR HIGH

Junior High Jitters
Class Crush
The Day the Eighth Grade Ran the School
How Dumb Can You Get?
The Eighth Grade to the Rescue
Eighth Grade Hero?
Those Crazy Class Pictures
Starring the Eighth Grade
Who's the Eighth Grade Hunk?
The Big Date
The Great Eighth Grade Switch
The Revolt of the Eighth Grade
Who's Haunting the Eighth Grade?

#13

JUNIOR HIGH

WHO'S HAUNTING THE EIGHTH GRADE?

Kate Kenyon

SCHOLASTIC INC.
New York Toronto London Auckland Sydney

ISBN 0-590-41787-8

12 11 10 9 8 7 6 5 4 3 2   8 9/8 0 1 2 3/9

Printed in the U.S.A.   01

First Scholastic printing, November 1988

Chapter 1

What's wrong with Mr. Rochester? the note said. Nora Ryan read it again, then looked across the classroom at the person who'd written it — her best friend, Jennifer Mann.

Jennifer was twisting a strand of her long dark hair around her finger, and there was a worried look in her hazel eyes.

Jen and her causes, Nora thought. Did the whales need saving? Jennifer joined the organization that was trying to do it. Did the elderly people in the nursing home need company? Jennifer visited them regularly, bringing cookies she'd baked herself. She was one of the most caring people Nora knew, and if something was wrong, Jennifer Mann would try to fix it.

But *was* there anything wrong with their English teacher? Nora gave Jennifer a puzzled shrug and then turned her attention to Mr. Rochester.

"Don't be afraid of Shakespeare," the handsome, black-eyed teacher was saying. "Don't even think of him as a 'great' writer. Try to think of him as a man who wrote about things all of us can understand — jealousy, rivalry, ambition, hate, love. . . ."

Nora's brown eyes narrowed as she watched him. She didn't care about William Shakespeare at the moment. She cared about Cliff Rochester. And Mr. Rochester was pale.

Not only was he pale, Nora thought, he was fidgety. He kept sticking his hands in his pockets, then taking them out. Then he'd fiddle with his tie for a second, look at the clock, drum his fingers on the desk, and stick his hands back in his pockets. He didn't seem interested in Shakespeare, either. Which was strange, because Mr. Rochester usually got so excited about every book or play or poem they had to read that he managed to get most of the class excited about it, too.

Nora looked over at Jennifer again. "Lunch," she mouthed, meaning she'd talk to Jen at lunch. She didn't know what was wrong, but Jen was right. Something was.

* * *

"It's too bad Cedar Groves doesn't have a medical library," Nora said later, while standing in the cafeteria line. She surveyed the hot food choices — macaroni glued together with cheese, or gray beef with semimashed potatoes — and settled on a salad, a corn muffin, and an orange. Then she glanced at Jennifer's tray. "You're not really going to eat that, are you?"

Jennifer looked at the Jell-O she'd just picked out. "I know it's mostly sugar," she admitted, "but at least it's got pieces of fruit in it."

"Canned fruit," Nora pointed out cheerfully. "Packed in heavy syrup."

"As bad as 'white death,' huh?" Jennifer asked. White death was Nora's term for refined sugar.

Nora nodded, her curly brown hair bouncing a little. She wanted to be a doctor — she'd known it since the third grade, when she'd found her first wounded bird — and she'd been giving everyone nutritional advice for just about that long, too. Fortunately, she had a sense of humor about it. "Go ahead," she told Jennifer now. "It's your body, your teeth, your blood sugar level — "

"And my taste buds, too," Jennifer interrupted with a laugh. "Come on, let's hurry, or

I won't even have time to eat any of it."

Balancing their trays, the two girls wove their way toward one of the big tables in the center of the crowded cafeteria. The eighth-graders always sat in the middle of the pea-soup-green room, and threw pitying looks at the seventh-graders, who had to sit at the narrow tables on the sidelines.

"Now," Jennifer said, plunking her tray down, "why do you wish Cedar Groves Junior High had a medical library? What I mean is, what does that have to do with Mr. Rochester?"

"Didn't you see how jittery he was?" Nora said. "There's usually a medical reason for that kind of thing."

"He didn't seem all that jittery to me," Jennifer said. "What I noticed was his eyes. They had a kind of funny, faraway look in them, like he just wasn't all there."

"That's a sign of stress, too," Nora told her. "Plus he was extremely pale."

"This definitely sounds serious," somebody said.

Nora and Jennifer looked up to find Lucy Armanson smiling down at them. As usual, the slender dark-eyed girl with the short Afro looked like a model from a fashion magazine.

Next to Lucy stood Denise Hendrix, another one of the most beautiful girls in the school, with silky blonde hair, a perfect figure, and enough clothes to fill ten closets. Her parents owned the international company, Denise Cosmetics, and Denise had spent many years in a Swiss boarding school and had traveled almost all over the world. Boys tended to trip over their own feet and behave like idiots when Denise was around, which she ignored in her coolest, most sophisticated manner.

"Who's pale and jittery?" Denise asked, sitting down and opening her juice carton.

"Mr. Rochester," Jennifer told her. "I think he's depressed, but Nora thinks he's sick."

"Nora's probably right," said Susan Hillard, who had just joined them.

Nora looked at her in surprise. Susan never took anybody's side. In fact, her main purpose in life seemed to be to disagree. But here she was, backing Nora. Had she finally gotten up on the right side of the bed?

"I noticed the way Mr. Rochester was acting," Susan went on, "and I say he's sick, too." She stuck a straw into her carton of apple juice and smiled. "Sick of teaching a class that's almost totally lacking in brainpower," she added sarcastically.

Nora rolled her eyes. So much for her theory about Susan's overnight personality change.

"See what I mean?" Susan said, before Nora

or anyone else had a chance to argue with her. "Look over there" — she pointed — "and tell me if you'd like to try teaching those two day after day."

Everybody looked and saw Mia Stevens and Tracy Douglas heading for the table. Mia, Cedar Groves' resident punk rocker, was wearing shiny orange pants that fit like a second skin, and an orange top with gold metallic threads in a pattern of lightning flashes zigzagging across it. Her hair stuck up from her head in a series of sharp green spikes, and from her earlobes dangled long, daggerlike pieces of gold that could have been registered as lethal weapons.

Behind the punk was the preppy — blonde haired, alligator-shirted Tracy, with every hair in place and both eyes on the lookout for boys.

"It's Heavy Metal and the Airhead," Susan remarked. "No wonder Mr. Rochester's been looking sick."

"Heavy Metal and the Airhead?" Tracy asked. "Is that a new group or what?"

"Or what," Jennifer said quickly, not wanting to give Susan a chance to put them down again. "Anyway, we were talking about Mr. Rochester."

"Oh, wow, that's really weird, you know?" Mia said. "I was just thinking about him."

6

"I never stop," Tracy sighed. "He's so gorgeous."

The others traded glances. When Mr. Rochester first came to Cedar Groves Junior High, most of the female population had developed an overwhelming crush on him. Tracy was obviously the only one who hadn't gotten over it yet.

"I wasn't thinking about him like that," Mia explained. "I was just trying to figure out where his head was today. He was so spacy, you know?"

"Exactly," Jennifer said, digging into her Jell-O. "Out of it, spacy, whatever. He just wasn't himself today. I think he's unhappy."

"And there's probably an underlying medical cause," Nora said. She pointed to the Ring-Ding Lucy had pulled out of her pocketbook. "Like poor diet."

"Please," Lucy laughed. "I eat a Ring-Ding almost every day, and I'm not unhappy."

"There's a definite relationship between nutrition and mood," Nora said.

"Right," Jennifer agreed, scooping up the last of her Jell-O. She grinned at Nora. "Cherry-flavored Jell-O is the reason I'm so cheerful."

"Ring-Dings and Twinkies for me," Lucy said.

Nora shook her head and laughed. "Don't say I didn't warn you," she said. "Just keep eating like that and one of these days you'll be as miserable as Mr. Rochester."

"Miserable?" Tracy took her eyes off a cute boy she'd spotted in the lunch line and frowned. "Gee, I didn't think he looked miserable. I thought he looked great. That burgundy sweater-vest was perfect with his dark eyes and hair."

Susan opened her mouth to say something sarcastic, but Jennifer jumped in first. "Tracy, we all agree he's handsome," she said gently. "But we were talking about his mood, not his looks."

"Oh." Tracy took a bite of apple and shrugged. "Well, I don't know. I saw him at the mall on Saturday and he was okay then. He and Ms. Spencer were coming out of the card shop and they were both laughing a lot. Of course, I guess something could have happened yesterday to make him miserable, but. . . ."

"Tracy, stop!" Jennifer cried. "Go back a sentence. You saw Mr. Rochester and *who* coming out of the card shop?"

"Ms. Spencer. You know, the new art teacher." Tracy took another bite of apple and looked around the table. Everyone was staring at her. "What's wrong?" she asked, patting her hair and glancing down at her blouse. "Did I spill something? Is there apple peel stuck in my braces?"

"Don't get frantic," Susan told her. "We weren't staring because of how you look. We're interested in what you said, for once."

"Really? What did I say?"

"About Mr. Rochester and Ms. Spencer," Denise reminded her.

"Oh, that. Oh!" Tracy's blue eyes opened wide. "You mean, you think it could be . . . the L word?"

Susan groaned. "It's not a bad word, Tracy. Go ahead and say it. Love."

"Wow!" Mia said. "I should have thought of that. Love can make you spacy."

"Hey, there she is," Jennifer said. "Ms. Spencer."

Unaware that she was the object of scrutiny by six girls, Allison Spencer, Cedar Groves' new art teacher, walked briskly across the cafeteria. She was tall and slender, with green eyes and light-brown hair that fell to her shoulders in soft, wavy curls.

"Well?" Susan said, when Ms. Spencer was out the door. "Does she look like she's in love?"

"I have her for art," Lucy said. "And she hasn't been acting strange at all. Maybe it's just guys who act weird when they're in love," she suggested. "Who do we know who's in love?"

"Well, there's Steve," Nora said, poking Jennifer and pointing across the room.

Jennifer grinned as they all looked at Steve Crowley, who had just come into the cafeteria. She and Nora had known him since kindergarten, and for a long time, she'd thought of him as a pal, someone she'd traded fingerpaints and crayons with. But then they'd gone on a date, and suddenly, Steve was more than just a buddy.

Steve caught Jennifer's eye and waved, a big smile lighting up his vivid blue eyes. She waved back, then got up and walked over to him. The others watched as the two of them talked together, holding hands and laughing.

"Steve's in love, all right," Lucy commented. "But he isn't acting strange. Just happy."

The others agreed and looked around the cafeteria again, trying to find evidence of strange, love-related behavior. Two tables down sat Mitch Pauley and Tommy Ryder. Mitch was a tall, dark-eyed boy who'd been voted the best all-around athlete in the class.

"Forget Mitch," Nora said. "He wouldn't know what love was unless it was written up in the sports section of the newspaper."

"Tommy knows about love," Denise laughed. "Every time he looks in the mirror, he tells himself how wonderful he is."

As if to prove her point, Tommy pulled a comb out of his back pocket and carefully ran it through his sandy brown hair.

"He *is* handsome." Tracy sighed. "And so is Mitch."

"I've got it," Susan said with a laugh. "How about Jason?"

At that moment, Jason Anthony, also known as the Terminal Creep and the Class Nerd, came speeding by on his skateboard. It was his main method of transportation at school, even though it was against the rules. A skinny, freckled redhead, Jason zipped close to the girls' table, stuck a bony finger into Lucy's half-eaten Ring-Ding, scooped out the creamy center, and pushed off.

"Yuck!" Tracy cried. "Totally gross!"

"So juvenile," Denise commented.

Lucy stared at the Ring-Ding. "Eating one of these will never make me happy again," she sighed.

Nora couldn't help laughing. "Okay, let's face it," she said. "The guys in our class won't be any help at all. If we want to find out whether Mr. Rochester and Ms. Spencer are in love, we're just going to have to do some detective work." She grinned. "And we'll call it 'Operation Loveseek.' "

Chapter 2

"Do you think we're being silly and juvenile?" Jennifer asked Nora after school that day.

The two of them were sitting in Temptations, Cedar Groves' popular ice cream parlor. Nora was having her usual Blueberry Yogurt Delight, and Jennifer was halfway through two scoops of chocolate ice cream smothered in crushed Oreos.

"Us? Silly and juvenile? Never," Nora said. "Anyway, silly and juvenile about what?"

"About Mr. Rochester and Ms. Spencer," Jennifer said. "I mean, if they're in love, that's their business, isn't it? Maybe we should just leave them alone."

Nora smiled. She'd been wondering the same thing herself, and she wasn't surprised that Jennifer had brought it up. They'd been best friends for so long, it seemed as if they could read each other's minds.

"Well," she said, "it's not like we're going to follow them around or anything. That would really be seventh-grade." She scooped the last blueberry out of her dish. "But there's absolutely nothing wrong with being interested."

Jennifer looked relieved. "I was hoping you'd say that."

"You *knew* I'd say that," Nora grinned. "Just think, Jen, there might be a great romance going on right under our noses."

"And I, for one, am dying to find out if there is," Jennifer said. "But how are we going to do it?"

The two friends looked at each other for a second. Then both of them spoke at the same time.

"Jeff!" they cried.

Twenty minutes later, Jennifer and Nora burst into the Manns' sparkling blue-and-white kitchen and found Jeff Crawford peering into the oven door at two loaves of baking French bread.

In his early fifties, with slightly graying hair and bright blue eyes, Jeff had been the Manns' housekeeper for two years. Jennifer's mother had died when Jen was very young, and after a parade of housekeepers for her and her younger brother, Eric, her father had finally found Jeff.

Jennifer knew that some people thought it was strange for a housekeeper to be a man, but it didn't bother her a bit. Not only was Jeff a great housekeeper, he was a great friend.

Nora liked him, too. He was logical and organized, just like she was. He also shared her opinion about the dangers of junk food.

"Unbleached flour?" Nora asked Jeff, pointing to the oven.

"Of course." Jeff closed the door and wiped his hands on his apron, which said LIFE IS UNCERTAIN, EAT DESSERT FIRST. It was a present from his girlfriend, Debby Kincaid, who had also knitted the sweater he was wearing. "Would I ever use anything else?"

"Never mind the dietary stuff now," Jennifer told him. "Nora and I have something very important to ask you."

"Ask away," Jeff said, folding his arms and leaning against the counter.

"Okay." Jennifer took a deep breath. "Is Cliff — Mr. Rochester — is he interested in anybody right now?"

Jeff raised his eyebrows. "Interested?"

"In love," Nora said bluntly.

Jeff's eyebrows shot up even farther.

"Please, don't tell me you're starting that again," he pleaded. "You know he's too old for you, and besides, I thought the class infatuation was a thing of the past."

Jennifer laughed. "Don't worry, it is. Nora and I no longer completely melt at the sight of his piercing black eyes."

"Right," Nora said, laughing, too. "We just partly melt."

Jeff breathed a sigh of relief. "I'm glad to hear it. But why this revival of interest?"

"We think he might be in love," Jennifer explained. "And we also thought you might be able to tell us about it."

"After all, you're from his hometown," Nora reminded Jeff. "He talks to you. I guess you're sort of like a father figure to him."

"Please." Jeff pretended to look insulted. "I suppose I am old enough to be his father, but I'd rather not be reminded of it."

"It was a compliment!" Nora assured him. "Anyway, what about it? Is Cliff — Mr. Rochester — in love with someone?"

"Someone named Allison Spencer?" Jennifer added.

Jeff took off his apron and hung it up in the broom closet. Then he faced the girls as if they were a firing squad. "I cannot tell a lie," he said.

"Great!" Jennifer cried. "We were counting on that!"

"Go ahead, Jeff," Nora urged. "Tell us the honest truth."

"The honest truth," Jeff said, his blue eyes twinkling, "is that I have absolutely *no knowledge* of Cliff Rochester's romantic attachments. I don't even have any idea whether he *has* a romantic attachment."

Nora looked at Jennifer. "He is telling the honest truth, isn't he?"

"I'm afraid so," Jen sighed.

Jeff smothered a laugh. "Cheer up," he advised. "If Cliff's in love, you'll find out sooner or later. In the meantime, have a cookie." He pointed to the ceramic Morris the Cat cookie jar on the counter. "Baked just this morning. Molasses, granola, almonds, and just a hint of coconut. I've christened them Coconolas."

Later that night, after she'd done her homework and taken a shower, Jennifer took two of Jeff's Coconolas with her to her room. She was skeptical about them — they felt like they weighed at least a pound apiece — but they turned out to be good. Not as good as chocolate chips, of course, but not bad, considering they were health cookies.

After polishing off the cookies, she got into her pink snuggly pajamas and then stood in front of the long mirror over her dressing table. She picked up her hairbrush and was just starting her nightly routine of a hundred strokes when the princess phone on her bedside table rang.

Jennifer grabbed the phone and stretched out on her white chenille bedspread. "Nora?"

It was Nora, of course. They talked to each other on the phone every night. It didn't matter if there was nothing important to talk about — half the time, they just rehashed what they'd done that day and discussed what they'd wear the next — what mattered was that they talk.

"What are you up to?" Nora asked.

"I was trying to decide whether to get my hair cut," Jennifer said. "And maybe get a perm."

"Well," Nora said thoughtfully, "you can do a lot of different things with your hair when it's long, I guess."

"But I don't," Jennifer sighed. "I just let it hang most of the time. Anyway, I wouldn't get it cut too short." She sat up and looked at her reflection across the room. "And it would be great to have some curls or waves. Right now, it looks like I iron it."

"Shoulder-length, wavy . . . hmm," Nora

said. "Sounds like a certain art teacher's hair."

"No, Ms. Spencer's is light brown, remember?" Jennifer laughed. "But you're right, I was thinking about her and Mr. Rochester."

"Me, too," Nora said. "And I remembered something that'll help us in Operation Loveseek — the parking lot."

Jennifer sat up, excited. "Of course! They both drive to school, so they've got to run into each other in the parking lot. If they're in love, they probably even plan it that way." Suddenly, she flopped back down. "But, Nora, we can't just hang out there, waiting to see them. It would be so obvious."

"Don't worry, I've thought of that, too," Nora said.

"I should have guessed," Jennifer teased. "Anyone who organizes her sweaters by texture and color wouldn't do sloppy detective work."

"Life's easier if you're organized," Nora replied, not insulted at all. "Anyway, here's the plan. This week is the senior bake sale to raise money for new sports equipment, right?"

"Right," Jennifer said.

"So we buy something every day after school and eat it on the steps by the parking lot," Nora explained. "And if we happen to see Mr. Rochester and Ms. Spencer together, well, so what? We won't look like we were waiting for them, we'll look perfectly casual and cool, just eating our granola bars, cupcakes or whatever and minding our own business."

For the next two days, Jennifer and Nora sat on the steps after school, chewing slowly and waiting patiently for a glimpse of Mr. Rochester and Ms. Spencer. They saw them both, but not together, which didn't count, of course.

"We'll give it one more try," Nora said on the third day. "Then we'll come up with another plan."

"Okay, but I'll kind of miss this," Jennifer said, unwrapping the butterscotch chip square she'd bought. "It's nice sitting out here, and the bake-sale food's a lot cheaper than Temptations."

"But at least Temptations has yogurt." Nora frowned at her slice of carrot cake. "This was the only thing I could find that was even vaguely nutritious," she said. "I should have made my Zucchini Bread Squares."

"No you shouldn't," Jennifer said quickly. Nora's efforts at cooking were usually disastrous; the only thing she really made well was homemade granola. "They want to raise money, not lose it, remember?"

Just then, the door opened behind them and they both looked around expectantly. It was Steve Crowley.

"Hi," he said. "Want some company?"

"Sure!" Jennifer gave him a big smile and scooted over to make room for him.

Steve sat down close to her and pulled out two waxed paper-wrapped brownies. The three of them munched quietly for a minute. Then Steve shook his head and chuckled.

"What's so funny?" Nora asked.

Steve chuckled again, his blue eyes sparkling. "I was just remembering when every girl in this class was acting like an idiot over Mr. Rochester."

Jennifer gave his arm a playful punch. "Please. That's completely in the past," she said. "We don't need to be reminded of it."

"Sorry, but it was so funny," Steve said, laughing even louder.

Nora punched him this time. Then she stared at him. "Wait a minute," she said. "We're all sitting here eating our bake-sale goodies, and you just happen to remember about Mr. Rochester? That doesn't make sense."

"She's right," Jennifer agreed. "What have

you been doing, just waiting until we thought everybody had forgotten about it so you could tease us again?"

Steve held up his hands. "I'm innocent, honest," he pleaded. "The reason I thought about it was because I saw Mr. Rochester this morning and it reminded me, that's all."

"Why should seeing him remind you of the way we all made dopes of ourselves?" Nora wanted to know.

"Well, because he wasn't alone," Steve said, taking a big bite of brownie.

Before Jennifer and Nora could ask who Mr. Rochester was with, the door opened again and Jason Anthony came out, a pile of cookies in one hand and his skateboard in the other.

"What's this?" he asked. "A picnic?" Without waiting for an answer, he dropped his skateboard next to Nora and sat down on it. "Mind if I join you?"

"You already did," Nora pointed out.

Steve swallowed the last of his brownie. "Well?" he asked the girls. "Don't you want to know who he was with?"

"Who?" Jason asked.

"Mr. Rochester," Steve said.

Jason looked confused. "Mr. Rochester was with Mr. Rochester?"

Jennifer sighed. "No, Jason, Mr. Rochester was with somebody else." She turned to Steve. "Tell us. Who?"

"I don't know her name," Steve said. "But I think she's the art teacher."

Jason nodded. "Ms. Spencer. Yeah, I saw them in Greatneck Park the other day."

Nora and Jennifer stared at him. "You saw them?" Nora asked.

"Together?" Jennifer asked.

"No, they were miles apart, but I have a split personality, so I saw them at the same time." Jason cackled at his idea of a witty remark.

"Extremely funny," Nora said. "So they were together. What were they doing?"

"Walking," Jason said. "What else do you do in the park?"

Nora and Jennifer looked at each other and rolled their eyes. Jason wouldn't recognize a romantic moment if it stared him in the face.

Completely oblivious to the significance of what he'd seen, Jason stretched out on his skateboard and bit into a popcorn ball.

Nora and Jennifer were trying to decide whether to give up and go home when the door opened again and Susan and Tracy came out, followed by Mitch and Tommy. Behind them came Mia and her boyfriend, Andy Warwick, the other half of Cedar Groves' punk duo. The two of them wore matching black jeans and green spiked hair, and Andy had on one of his many dog collars — black leather with pointed silver studs.

"Hey, what's happening?" Andy asked. "Where's the action?"

"Not here, that's for sure," Nora told him.

"Don't tell me," Susan said. "You two have been sitting here waiting to see if Mr. Rochester and Ms. Spencer come out together." She laughed and shook her head. "What a waste of time. I saw them yesterday afternoon at the Briarpatch. They were looking at a volume of Shakespeare."

"Oh, yeah, I just remembered," Mia said, flicking up a drooping green spike with one of her burgundy-colored fingernails. "Andy and I saw them at the record store together. They were in the pop section." She sighed with disappointment. "I always thought Mr. Rochester went in for my kind of music, but I guess love has corrupted his taste."

"Improved it, you mean," Susan said.

Mitch looked a little confused. "Hey, what are you guys talking about? You think there's something going on between those two?"

"Between Mr. Rochester and Ms. Spencer?" Tommy asked, smoothing back his hair. "I don't know. You really think he's her type?"

Nora rolled her eyes again. Tommy Ryder thought there was only one type that was attractive to females — his.

Jennifer wadded her empty waxed paper into a ball and stood up. Operation Loveseek had been a success, for everybody but her and Nora. All she had to show for it was the threat of acne on her chin from three days' worth of cupcakes and cookies. Of course, nobody had any real proof that the two teachers were in love. But if they were, then she'd find out soon enough, like Jeff said.

Jennifer started to say she was going home, when suddenly Nora elbowed her in the ribs.

"Look!" Nora whispered.

Jennifer looked, and so did everyone else. Around the corner of the building, unaware that they had an audience, came the two objects of Operation Loveseek. They strolled into the parking lot, and as the congregation of eighth-graders watched silently from the steps, Mr. Rochester reached out and took Ms. Spencer's hand.

"Oh, wow," Mia breathed quietly.

Tracy sighed. "Isn't it romantic?"

"Gee," Jason said, balancing on one foot on his skateboard, "I just remembered — they were holding hands in Greatneck Park, too."

Nora burst out laughing. "*Now* he tells us!"

Chapter 3

Dear Diary, Jennifer wrote later that night. *Big news! Mr. Rochester and Ms. Spencer are definitely in love. When two teachers hold hands in the school parking lot, you can be pretty sure it's not just friendship!*

We're all excited about it. All the girls, that is. Some of the boys think it's corny. But as Nora says, boys (not Steve) mature much more slowly than girls. Jason Anthony sure proves that!

Jennifer stretched and yawned, then got up from her red beanbag chair and took the diary over to her bed.

I'm really tired tonight, so I'm not going to write anymore — except to say that I'm glad Operation Loveseek is over. My complexion wouldn't have been able to take many more cupcakes! Your friend, Jennifer.

Even though Operation Loveseek was over, since love had been sought and found, the new romance was still the main topic of conversation.

"Isn't it romantic?" Tracy said again at lunch the day after the hand-holding incident. "I wonder if it was love at first sight?"

"Oh, isn't it romantic?" someone squeaked in a high falsetto.

Tracy, Susan, Jen, Nora, Mia, and Denise turned to see Tommy and Mitch passing their table.

"Oh, Romeo, Romeo!" Tommy squeaked. "Speak now or forever hold your peace!" Almost collapsing in laughter, the two boys wove their way to another table.

"Good grief, they can't even quote it right," Susan remarked.

"Quote what?" Tracy asked, looking blank.

"*Romeo and Juliet*," Susan told her with a sigh.

"Is that our assignment?" Tracy asked in a panicked voice. "I thought it was *Macbeth*!"

Before Susan could come up with a withering remark, Jennifer quickly explained that Mitch and Tommy had been saying some lines from

26

another one of Shakespeare's plays, but they'd gotten them wrong. "They're just acting that way because they're embarrassed," she said. "They'd die before they'd admit they're interested in the romance, too."

"Oh." Tracy looked relieved. "Well, anyway, do you think it was love at first sight?"

"Probably not," Denise said. "I don't think it happens that way very often."

"It happened that way with Andy and me," Mia said dreamily. "We both came to school one day with half our hair dyed purple and when we saw each other in the halls, it was like. . . ."

Mia stopped, unable to think of the right word. Nobody else could think of it, either.

"Well, anyway," Denise said, after a pause, "Ms. Spencer seems too levelheaded to fall in love like that. I get the idea in art class that she's a both-feet-on-the-ground type."

"Unlike some people we know." Nora pointed at Jason, who was careening through the cafeteria at a dangerous speed.

As the skateboard neared the girls' table, Jason grinned and stretched out one long, skinny arm.

"Jason Anthony, if you stick your finger in my food, I'm going to scream!" Tracy shrieked.

Still grinning, Jason maneuvered the skateboard behind Tracy, who was desperately trying to cover three dishes with two hands. The apple cobbler was left out in the open, and Jason neatly swiped the crust as he flashed by.

True to her word, Tracy screamed.

"Face it!" Jason called out in passing, "what would you do without me?"

"We'd stop gagging, for one thing!" Susan called after him.

While Tracy was staring glumly at her decapitated cobbler, Lucy dropped by the table. She'd been out with a cold for two days, and even though she looked great in her royal blue sweater, black skirt, and gold hoop earrings, she was still sniffling.

"There's absolutely nothing worse than a head cold," she commented. "And having a father who's a doctor doesn't help. He just says 'If you wait long enough, it'll go away.' So I drank at least a gallon of hot tea, and it didn't help a bit. My head still feels like it's full of cotton." She grinned at Nora. "Have *you* got any suggestions, Dr. Ryan?"

Nora grinned back. She loved the sound of that title. "You're not going to believe this, but chicken soup is actually supposed to help the symptoms of the common cold."

"You're right. I don't believe it, but I'm willing to try anything," Lucy laughed.

"Hey, we've got to catch you up on what's been happening in Operation Loveseek," Jennifer said, and quickly gave Lucy a detailed description of everything they'd seen.

"Isn't that just so incredibly *neat*?" Tracy asked when Jennifer had finished.

Lucy nodded, and started to say something, but Mia broke in.

"I wonder if it's really serious," she said, "or just a short-term thing, you know?"

"Oh, it's serious all right," Lucy said. "They're getting married."

Everyone stared at her, speechless. Tracy gasped, and even Susan couldn't think of anything sarcastic to say for a moment. Finally, though, Susan recovered. Lucy always seemed to know things before anyone else did, and it really bugged her. "You've been out sick for two days," she reminded Lucy. "How could you find out something like that? You don't even have Mr. Rochester for English."

"No, but I have Ms. Spencer for art, first thing in the morning," Lucy said. She was about the only one who could take Susan on and come out on top. "And this cold doesn't bother my eyesight one bit. So when I saw that pretty diamond ring on the third finger of Ms. Spencer's left hand, I put two and two together and heard wedding bells."

"Here's something to consider about Lady Macbeth," Mr. Rochester told the class on Monday. "Was she acting out of love for her husband? Or was she simply a cold-hearted woman whose ruthlessness finally caught up with her? And what about Macbeth himself? What kind of man was he?"

"Simple. He was a wimp," Mitch declared. "His wife says 'Kill the guy,' and he says, 'Yes, dear.'"

Since it was something of a phenomenon for Mitch Pauley to make any comment at all, Mr. Rochester decided to go easy on him. "Well, that's one way of looking at it, I guess," he said. "But I think if you read some of the scenes again you'll find that explanation a little too simple."

"Just like Mitch's brain," Susan commented under her breath to Nora.

"Now," Mr. Rochester went on, "we've only got a few more minutes left, and I want to make an announcement."

Tracy giggled and waved her hand in the air. "We know, Mr. Rochester," she said. "You're engaged to be married. And we think it's just incredible!"

The handsome teacher came as close to blushing as anyone had ever seen him. "Well . . . ah . . . yes, as a matter of fact, Tracy, you're right," he said. "I am engaged."

Some of the boys groaned. "So you're really going to tie the knot, huh?" Tommy said. "Are you sure you really want to? I mean, it does narrow down the field." He laughed and gave his imitation of a sophisticated leer.

Jennifer wanted to die. Sometimes it was embarrassing to be in the same room with somebody as juvenile as Tommy Ryder. She raised her hand.

"Yes, Jennifer," Mr. Rochester said.

"I just wanted to say congratulations," Jennifer told him. "We all hope you'll be very happy."

"Right, and Mr. Rochester," Mia said. "If you haven't picked your wedding music yet, I've got some great tapes you could listen to. Don't worry," she added, "the stuff's not too punk."

"Well, thanks, Mia." Mr. Rochester laughed. "But we haven't set a date yet."

"Oh, make it a spring wedding!" Tracy urged excitedly.

"Uh, yes, we'll see what we can do," the teacher said. "Anyway, on to the announcement."

"Another one?" Jason asked.

"The one he was going to make before Tracy got carried away," Susan said.

"That's okay, Tracy," Mr. Rochester said, seeing her look of embarrassment. "I'm kind of excited about it myself. But," he went on, "what I wanted to tell all of you was that the Tri-State Repertory Company in Rockford just opened its production of *Macbeth*, and I've arranged for the class to go see it."

"A field trip!" Mitch said. "Now that's the kind of announcement I like to hear!"

"It's an overnighter," Mr. Rochester said, as he began to pass out permission slips. "We'll leave Friday after school, see that night's performance, stay in a hotel in Rockford, and get back to Cedar Groves early Saturday afternoon."

Nora glanced at the permission slip. It said pretty much what Mr. Rochester had just told them, except for one very important thing. The second faculty member to go with them wasn't Mrs. Hogan, the drama teacher, as Nora expected. It was Ms. Allison Spencer, the art teacher.

* * *

"So, since Mrs. Hogan already made plans to visit some relatives this weekend," Nora explained to her sister, Sally, "Ms. Spencer's going to come and tell us all about the set design."

It was Thursday night, and Nora was busy packing a batch of her homemade granola to take on the trip. She knew she'd get hungry, and she didn't want to be at the mercy of the fast-food monopoly.

"Set design, huh?" Sally said knowingly. She was a freshman at the university, and she should have been studying. But since what she really wanted to do was be a dancer, she was in the Ryans' kitchen, using the counter as a barre. "That's nice and convenient for the two lovebirds."

Nora's mother, Jessica, glanced up. A Legal Aid lawyer, she spent most of her evenings at the kitchen table, trying to dig her way out from under the mountainous backlog of paperwork. "Your father's a little concerned about this trip," she said to Nora. "I think he's worried that 'the two lovebirds' will neglect their duties to their students."

"Oh, that's ridiculous," Nora snorted, putting granola into a plastic bag. "They're grown-ups."

"Grown-ups have been known to behave a little strangely when they fall in love." Mrs.

Ryan smiled. "I'm not worried about that at all, though. I just hope the rest of you give them a little privacy once in a while. I remember when one of my high school teachers got engaged, we dogged her trail like hounds, hoping we'd see her kiss her fiance."

"Mother!" Nora looked indignant. "That was ages ago. Kids are much more sophisticated now."

Mrs. Ryan smiled again and started to say something, but the phone interrupted her.

"I'll get it!" Nora cried, dashing out of the kitchen. "It's for me!"

In her room, Nora grabbed the phone off her nightstand on the third ring. "Jennifer?"

"Who else?" Jennifer said. "It's me, and I can't decide what to take for the play. What are you wearing?"

Nora consulted her checklist. She always made one, even for a picnic in Greatneck Park. "My burgundy jumpsuit, the one with the braided belt," she told Jennifer. "Why don't you wear your new cherry-red one? You look great in that color."

"That's what I want to take," Jennifer said, lowering her voice. "But Dad just bought me a dress, and he sort of hinted that it would be a great thing to wear to a play."

Nora was silent. Jennifer's father was very

generous; he was constantly buying her clothes whenever something caught his eye. And what usually caught his eye was great — for an eight-year-old. "What is it this time?" she asked.

"Pink," Jennifer said disgustedly. "With a lace collar. I'm surprised he didn't buy me a pair of Mary Janes to go with it."

"Look, pack it anyway," Nora advised. "That way you can tell him you took it. What you won't tell him is that it never left your suitcase."

"Great, you've solved my problem," Jennifer said. "What would I do without you?"

Nora laughed. "You'd go around in pink lacy dresses and patent leather shoes," she teased. "Guess what?"

"What?"

"My dad's worried that Mr. Rochester and Ms. Spencer are going to sneak a few kisses on this trip and my mom's worried that we're going to try to catch them at it."

"Oh, that's ridiculous," Jennifer said. Actually, she'd been thinking about the same thing. "We wouldn't do anything like that."

"That's what I said. Of course," Nora added, "if they do happen to kiss, and we just happen to see it, well. . . ." she smiled into the phone, "It would be kind of fun, wouldn't it?"

"Fun?" Jennifer giggled, "in Tracy's words, it would be just absolutely, incredibly romantic!"

Chapter 4

On Friday morning, Jennifer woke ten minutes ahead of her alarm clock, which was nothing short of a miracle. True, she was excited about the trip, but not excited enough to give up ten minutes of sleep. She snuggled back down under her pink comforter and snoozed for fifteen more minutes. When she woke up, it wasn't because of her alarm, which had obviously died again. Lying there, fiddling with the clock, she suddenly realized what had made her wake up in the first place.

It was raining. Not a nice, soothing pitter-patter, either, but a crashing, driving rain that beat against her window like bullets.

"It isn't going to last," Jeff assured her when she came into the kitchen with her duffel bag. "The weather report says it should level off by noon."

"Level off?" Jennifer asked, pouring herself some orange juice. "Not stop?"

"No, I'm afraid it's supposed to be an all-day affair," he said. "But your field trip should go on as scheduled, so cheer up."

"I'm not worried about the trip, at least not yet," Jennifer told him, gulping down the juice. "I'm worried about missing the bus."

"But you're right on time," Jeff said.

"I know, but when it's raining, the bus driver's always early." Jennifer ran into the hall and started searching through the closet. "You'd think he'd be late when the weather's bad," she called back over her shoulder, "but this guy takes his job very seriously and gets a head start."

"A commendable habit," Jeff said, following her into the hall.

"I know, I know," she muttered, pawing through the coats. "Nora thinks it's great, too, naturally."

Jeff laughed. "What on earth are you looking for?"

"My poncho. . . . Oh, no!" Jennifer wailed. "I forgot, it's got that tear in it and I still haven't sewn it up." She gave Jeff a stern look. "Don't you dare say anything about being organized."

Jeff held up his hand. "I wasn't going to say

a word," he protested. "Except I hope you have a delightful trip, and give my regards to Willie."

"Who's Willie?"

"Willie S." Jeff's blue eyes crinkled in laughter. "William Shakespeare."

"I would have gotten that if I hadn't been in such a hurry." Jennifer struggled into her only other raincoat — a hooded plastic slicker the same color as the school bus. Like all her father's other purchases, it made her look at least six years younger.

Jeff kept a straight face while she snapped it up, and Jennifer was grateful. Just as she was about to dash out the door, he handed her a small shopping bag. "What's in it?" she asked, hefting it in her hand. "Bricks?"

"Bite your tongue," he said. "It's a full day's supply of my Coconolas. In case you get hungry on the bus."

When Jennifer joined the other eighth-graders waiting on the front steps, she was puffing from the weight of her duffel bag and the Coconolas. It was still raining, although not quite as hard.

"Sometimes I think this tradition of staying on the steps until the last bell should be abolished," she complained to Nora.

Nora, she noticed, was looking calm and collected, and prepared. She had an umbrella as well as her poncho. The poncho was exactly like Jennifer's except Jennifer's was red and Nora's was blue. Also, Nora's wasn't torn. If it had been, she would have sewn it up the very second she discovered it.

Like Jeff, Nora didn't say anything about Jennifer's yellow slicker. She knew how much her friend hated it. She could also tell by the look on Jen's face that she'd had to rush for the bus. "Bad start?" she asked sympathetically.

Jennifer nodded glumly. "My alarm broke, I had to run for the bus, I had to carry my duffel bag and a bag of Jeff's cookies, which weighs at least twenty-five pounds, and my poncho's ripped so I had to wear this." She took a deep breath. "If anybody says one word about this raincoat, I'm going to scream."

"Don't worry," Nora assured her. "Susan's the only one who'd say anything. Hey, why don't I just say it for her and get it over with?" She glanced around and then in a voice very much like Susan's, she said, "Honestly, Jennifer, I thought for sure you would have buried that thing by now!"

A moment later, Susan came up the steps, looked Jennifer up and down and said, "Honestly, Jennifer, I thought for sure you would have buried that thing by now!"

Just then, the second bell rang, and Jennifer went into school with a smile on her face.

Later in the day, it was Jennifer's turn to cheer Nora up. She was waiting in the lunch line with Lucy, trying to decide between the spaghetti and the chicken à la king, when she spotted Nora in the door to the cafeteria. Her friend had a notebook clutched to her chest and a panicked look in her brown eyes.

"What is it?" Jennifer asked, when Nora had hurried over to them.

"Don't ask," Nora said.

Lucy smiled. "Do you really mean that?"

"No, I guess I might as well share my misery," Nora told them. She took a deep breath and lowered the notebook. Across the front of her salmon-colored cotton sweater was a dark splotch shaped something like an octopus. "Please," she begged, "say you'd hardly notice it."

Jennifer took a deep breath, too. "You'd hardly notice it," she said faintly.

"Notice what?" Lucy asked innocently.

"You two are terrible liars," Nora moaned, "but thanks for trying."

"What is it we're not supposed to be noticing?" Lucy asked, handing Nora a metal tray.

"It's oil!" Nora cried. "Jason was oiling his skateboard wheels and he asked me to steady it for him. It seemed like a simple thing to do."

"Nothing's simple when Jason's involved," Jennifer said.

"I know, I must have had a memory lapse," Nora moaned. "Anyway, the worst part is, it wasn't even his fault. The oil can got stopped up and I took it and — "

"Decorated your sweater," Lucy finished.

Nora nodded miserably. "Jason griped at me for wasting the oil, can you believe it? Then Tommy came by and did his imitation of Lady Macbeth — 'Out, out, damn'd spot.' And here's the absolute worst part," she finished, "I didn't bring another top."

Jennifer was speechless. Nora, the queen of organizers, forgetting to pack extra clothes, just in case?

"Go ahead and laugh," Nora said. In her agitated state, she'd actually taken a serving of the chicken à la king, which she claimed was dangerously full of cholesterol. "I had a second sweater all picked out, but I forgot to put it on my checklist, and I never packed it."

"Never mind," Jennifer said, recovering her powers of speech. "My bag's in my locker, but here." She was wearing an orange turtleneck under a chocolate brown sleeveless sweater vest. She put down her tray and quickly pulled the vest over her head and handed it to Nora.

"Put this on. It'll cover that, um, design, and nobody'll know the difference. Later," she teased, "you can borrow my pink dress if you want."

"I'm not that desperate, Jen," Nora laughed, gratefully pulling on the vest. How lucky she was to have a best friend like Jennifer, she thought. Who else would give her the sweater off her back? Then Nora stared at the gravy-smothered chunks of chicken on her tray on the table. "Who put that disgusting stuff there?"

"You did," Lucy laughed. "Another memory lapse."

"Maybe it's the weather," Jennifer suggested. "This is turning out to be one of those days."

It seemed to be one of those days for just about everybody. By the time they gathered on the front steps after school, Andy and Mia had argued about which punk rock group was the best and weren't speaking; Denise was brooding because Timothy Marks, the boy she liked, hadn't called her in five days, Jason was complaining that Nora had wasted all the oil his skateboard wheels needed, and even Lucy, who was usually unflappable, got slightly flapped when her combination lock stuck and she had to get the custodian to break into her locker so she could get her overnight bag.

"I was afraid you'd already be gone," she said breathlessly, finally joining the others on the front steps.

"We wouldn't do that," Tracy said.

"We couldn't do that," Susan snapped. "The bus is late."

Lucy shook her head and decided not to get into it with Susan. That girl must have spent all day sharpening her tongue, she thought.

"This is going to be so much fun!" Tracy bubbled. She didn't quite understand why everyone else was so grumpy. A little rain couldn't get her down. She had a brand-new sweater to wear, a soft peach color that went perfectly with her complexion and her silky blonde hair. Plus, Mitch and Tommy were here, and they were so cute, and to ride on the bus with them for three hours would be heavenly. She couldn't wait to get going.

Tracy had to wait, though. They all did. The bus was supposed to be there at five minutes after three. Fifteen minutes later, it still hadn't shown up. As Jeff and the weather forecaster had predicted, the rain had leveled off — instead of thundering down in torrents, it now just poured down at a cold, steady pace.

"This *is* where we were supposed to wait,

isn't it?" Steve asked, putting his arm around Jennifer.

Mitch nodded. "That's what the permission slip said." His dark hair was wet, and he had to keep blinking raindrops off his eyelashes. "Bus 184, main entrance."

"Incredible!" Susan said to no one in particular. "He can read!"

"Susan, why don't you just dry up?" Nora suggested. She wasn't crazy about Mitch, but at the moment she was even less crazy about Susan.

"That's kind of hard to do in the pouring rain," Susan shot back.

"Oh, please, you two," Tracy said anxiously. "Don't fight. This is supposed to be fun!"

"Tracy's right," Jennifer said. "We're just grouchy because we're wet. I say everybody keep their mouths shut until we get on the bus."

"Yeah, but what bus?" Tommy asked, carefully checking his hair.

"That one!" Jason stood up, pointing a long arm toward the end of the drive. "Bus 184, at our service!"

"At last!" Tracy said. "Now we can have a good time!"

Gathering up their duffel bags and overnight cases, the group made its way down the steps, ready to get on the bus the minute it stopped.

But the bus didn't stop. Instead of taking the curve to the front of the school, it kept going straight, heading for the back.

"Methinks I've had enough waiting around," Jason announced. He pulled on his poncho, which he'd been using to keep his skateboard dry, tossed back his mop of wet red hair, and zoomed off after the bus.

Jennifer laughed. "Methinks he has the right idea," she said, and took Steve's hand. "Come on, let's go!"

Damp and bedraggled, but finally united in their urge to catch the bus, the group dashed off after Jason. He was far ahead of them, and so close to the bus that he was getting drenched by the spray from its wheels. Finally, though, the bus pulled away from him, rounded another curve and was out of sight.

Jason stopped, turned around, and held out his hands. "I really needed that oil, Nora!" he shouted. "If the wheels were oiled, I would have caught him!"

"What's he talking about?" Susan asked.

Nora was laughing and pink-cheeked from the run. "I spilled some of his oil," she said, deciding not to say where she'd spilled it. "Do you suppose he's going to blame me forever?"

"No, that's one good thing about Jason," Susan said. "He doesn't hold a grudge."

Nora looked at her, waiting.

"He can't remember things long enough to hold a grudge," Susan added dryly. Then she smiled a little. "I couldn't resist saying that."

"I didn't think you could," Nora told her. But she was still laughing, and her grumpiness was gone.

"But what about the bus?" Tracy wailed. "What are we going to do? It just disappeared!"

"No, it didn't," Denise said, pointing. "Here it comes."

Sure enough, the bus was back in sight, heading toward them this time. Jason kicked up his skateboard and ran to join the others as they stood by the side of the drive, waving and shouting for it to stop.

It stopped, all right, screeching to a halt right in the middle of an enormous puddle of water, which flew up from the wheels and completely drenched the entire group.

The driver opened the doors, apologizing for the shower he'd given them. Then Mr. Rochester and Ms. Spencer appeared in the doorway, barely glancing at the half-drowned group of students waiting to get on. They only had eyes for each other. And their eyes were flashing.

"You said you'd take care of it," Mr. Rochester was saying.

"I said no such thing," Ms. Spencer protested. "You said the bus was going to pick them up at the side entrance and I reminded you that the permission slip said the front entrance and that's the way we left it. Since you made the change, I naturally thought you'd inform everybody of it."

"I didn't make the change," Mr. Rochester told her. "The bus company did."

"That's beside the point," she said quickly.

"You're right," he agreed. "The point is, you said — "

"I did not — "

"Hey, you two," the bus driver interrupted cheerfully. "You want to forget the point and let these kids on?"

Suddenly aware of their audience, the two teachers clammed up and stepped back out of the way. Avoiding each others' eyes, they smiled somewhat grimly at the students.

"Well," Jennifer whispered, as she and Nora made their way down the aisle of the bus, "it looks like we're not the only ones who had a bad day."

Chapter 5

Once everyone had stowed their bags and settled into seats, the bus finally pulled away from Cedar Groves. As it did, the rain stopped completely, the sky lightened from dark to pale gray, and everybody's mood lightened with it.

"It's the Shakespeare Express!" Jason shouted when they passed the city limits sign. He was toweling his skateboard dry with a T-shirt. "And we're off!"

The bus pulled to the side of the road and stopped.

"I *thought* we were off," Jason added.

"We were," Nora said. "I wonder what the problem is."

Mitch put his hand to his mouth and gave a piercing whistle. "Let's get this show on the road!" he called.

"It's not the driver's fault," Jennifer told him. "Stop breaking our eardrums with that whistling and listen."

Mitch listened. So did everybody else, except for Mia, who'd put on her Walkman the minute she sat down and was tapping her knees to the beat of X, the best punk group, no matter what Andy said.

"If we take Route Seven," Ms. Spencer was saying, "we'll hit all that traffic from the computer plant. The four o'clock shift will be coming out just as we get there."

"I know," Mr. Rochester said, trying to sound patient, "but Route Seven-A goes through too many towns. We'll get caught in local traffic in every one of them. And I happen to know there's a one-lane detour on Seven-A."

"Gee, they sound just like my parents," Tracy whispered to Denise. "Every time we get in the car to go somewhere, Mom and Dad argue about which route to take." She shook her head, her blue eyes confused. "I never thought an engaged couple would care about things like that, though."

"I didn't, either," Denise admitted. "At least, not a couple who's only been engaged for a week."

Tommy leaned over the back of their seat.

"Looks like the romance is wearing off, huh?" He grinned. "What do you think, girls? Do you think I'm Allison's type?"

Denise gave him a cool look. "Tommy, even if you were thirteen years older, you wouldn't be Ms. Spencer's type. She has very good taste, you know."

Undaunted, Tommy settled back in his seat. At least Denise had looked at him. And one of these days, he was sure she'd like what she saw.

Meanwhile, the two teachers were still bickering about which highway to take. Ms. Spencer, looking very stylish in a pair of tan pleated pants and a dark green, cowl-necked sweater that matched her eyes, put her hands on her hips. "What do you suggest we do?" she asked Mr. Rochester. "Flip a coin?"

"No," he said in a clipped voice. "I suggest we take Route Seven."

"It's a stand-off," Steve whispered to Jennifer.

"I hope not," Jennifer whispered back. "I was kind of hoping to see *Macbeth*."

"Why bother?" Susan said from the seat behind, which she was sharing with Mia. "There's plenty of drama right here."

"Yeah, but it's even more boring than Shakespeare," Mitch complained. Actually, he'd decided that *Macbeth* was pretty good stuff — at least, the parts he understood. But he wasn't about to admit it.

Finally, the bus driver, whose name was Frank, came to the rescue. "Listen folks," he said. "Anybody got any objections to Route Nine? No construction, no computer plants, and only one little town between here and Rockford." He checked his watch and smiled at the teachers. "If we get going now, you might make it in time to see your play. How does that sound?"

It sounded good to everybody, even Mr. Rochester and Ms. Spencer, who settled back in their seats as the bus once more drove off.

"Different seats, you notice," Jennifer said across the aisle to Nora. Her forehead was puckered with worry lines and her hazel eyes were anxious. "Do you think they're really mad at each other?"

"If they are, they'll cool off," Nora said. Give Jen a chance, she thought, and she'd worry about everyone in the world. "Come on, let's eat something. I'm starving."

Jennifer eagerly passed around Jeff's Coconolas, but even though everybody had one, the bag still weighed a ton. "Come on," she pleaded, "take two. I don't want to have to carry this bag home."

"I think Jeff must have had something else on his mind when he made these," Nora said. "They taste great, but they sink to the bottom of your stomach and stay there. Sort of like an anchor."

"You could always use a couple of them as a doorstop," Steve suggested. His father owned a restaurant, and Steve prided himself on his own culinary abilities. "Now take my meringue cookies," he said, "they're light as a feather."

"Maybe you'll give Jeff the recipe," Jennifer said hopefully.

Nora shook her head. "Too sweet," she said. "Jeff knows his health food."

"I'll eat one any time you make them, Steve," Lucy told him.

"Me, too," Jennifer agreed.

Nora couldn't help laughing. "You guys are hopeless."

Jason heard them laughing, but he couldn't make himself join in. He was nervous. This was only the second field trip he'd been on, and the first one had been a disaster. He'd humiliated himself in front of everybody by getting home-sick and almost crying. What if the same thing happened this time? He didn't want it to, but you never knew about feelings. They had a way of creeping up on you.

Swallowing dryly, Jason spun the wheels of

his skateboard, sending a little spray of water onto Andy's spiked hair, which had a greenish-bronze stripe running through the middle of it.

"Watch the water," Andy said, fingering his hair. "I just got this back in shape after the rain."

"Sorry." Jason swallowed again and glanced around. Jennifer was looking at him. He tried to think of something extremely clever to say, but before he could, she gave him a big smile and a thumbs-up sign. It was almost like she knew he was nervous and was trying to cheer him on. Was she a mind-reader? Well, if she was, at least he could count on her not to blab to everybody else. But he decided he'd better try to keep his thoughts to himself from now on. He gave Jennifer a lopsided grin and settled back in his seat, suddenly feeling better.

Tracy was feeling great. Denise was sound asleep beside her — she even looked beautiful with her cheek scrunched up against the seat-back — so Tracy had Tommy Ryder all to herself.

Tommy was so cute, Tracy thought. She liked the way his eyes lit up when he smiled. He was telling her how he planned to go back-stage at the play's intermission.

"You never know," he said. "Actors always take their agents with them. And agents are always on the lookout for new talent. I just might get discovered."

"That would be fantastic," Tracy agreed breathlessly. Deep in her heart, she knew Tommy was not going to get discovered backstage at *Macbeth*, but she wasn't about to tell him that. He was paying attention to her, so why spoil it with the truth?

Next to Tracy, Denise heard Tommy droning on and on, and tried not to laugh. He was so full of himself. She'd pretended to go to sleep just so she wouldn't have to talk to him. She wanted to think about Timothy, and why he hadn't called.

There was really no reason, not that she could think of. They hadn't argued or anything. So why hadn't he called her?

"Oh, that sounds so exciting!" Tracy cooed to Tommy.

Denise smothered a smile. Tracy was nice, but the way she acted around boys was about fifty years behind the times. But then, Denise thought suddenly, so is sitting around waiting for the phone to ring. This is the 1980's, she told herself, and you're a modern girl. Everybody thinks you're sophisticated and worldly, so act that way. If you want to talk to him, why don't you call him?

It was a very simple solution, and the minute

Denise thought of it, she really did fall asleep. After all the traveling she'd done, she'd finally decided that the easiest way to reach your destination was to sleep until you got there.

Halfway to Rockford, the rain started up again, beating a steady tattoo on the roof of the bus.

"Looks like we're chasing this storm," the driver remarked. "But don't worry, I'll get you there in time for your play. What is it, anyway?"

"*Macbeth*," Mr. Rochester said. "Probably Shakespeare's greatest tragedy."

"Not counting *King Lear*," Ms. Spencer added.

Mr. Rochester looked at her. They were sitting just in front of the students, across the aisle from each other. "No," he said. "Counting *King Lear*."

"Uh-oh," Nora said softly.

Ms. Spencer laughed. "Well, I know I'm not an authority, but there are plenty of Shakespearean scholars who would disagree with you."

"Trouble," Lucy whispered.

"True," Mr. Rochester said, "but there are even more who'd agree with me. I can name several, if you like."

"Please don't," she said. "When it comes to

Shakespearean scholars, I can't name-drop as well as you."

"Maybe that's because you teach art, not English," he told her.

Jason whistled under his breath. " 'Double, double, toil and trouble,' " he said, quoting the witches from *Macbeth*.

" 'Fire burn and cauldron bubble,' " Steve went on.

"Ssh!" Jennifer hissed. "They'll hear you!"

"No they won't," Susan told her. "They're too busy being mad at each other."

"Look, Cliff," Ms. Spencer was saying, "just because you're the English teacher doesn't make you the authority. My opinion's perfectly valid, and you know it."

"Sure, Al, it's valid. . . ."

"He calls her 'Al'!" Tracy squeaked.

". . . it's also flawed," Mr. Rochester finished.

" 'Double, double . . .' " Jason muttered again.

"Jason!" Tracy cried.

"It's my favorite part!" he protested loudly.

Denise woke with a start. "What's going on?" she asked, yawning and blinking her eyes.

"An argument," Tracy whispered to her. "Mr. Rochester and Ms. Spencer are still at it, and Jason thinks it's funny."

"Well, it isn't exactly a tragedy, either," Susan said. "They're acting more like seventh-graders than seventh-graders."

"I didn't mean that," Denise said. "I mean what's going on with the bus? It made a weird sound. That's what woke me up."

"There's nothing weird about this bus except some of the people in it," Susan commented.

But nobody answered, because, at that moment, everybody heard the same thing Denise had. Not only was it weird, it was loud, a wild, thumping, metallic sound, as if someone had thrown a pair of tap shoes into a clothes dryer.

Even Mia heard it. She took off her earphones, listened a second, and then looked relieved. "Wow, for a minute there, I thought X was using hammers in that last song."

The two teachers stopped glaring at each other and looked at the driver. So did everyone else. But the driver was too busy to say anything. Gripping the big wheel tightly, he started easing the bus onto the shoulder of the road. The thumping noises reached a crescendo, and suddenly, the engine died.

Slowly and silently, the bus coasted to a stop.

Chapter 6

"I vote that we go back and start this day all over again," Jennifer said, as the driver pulled on his rain slicker and went outside to inspect the engine. "All those in favor?"

Lucy laughed. "Somehow, I don't think it's going to be possible, not unless you've got a magical flying carpet."

"Hah, hah!" Jason grinned and held up his skateboard. "It's not magic, but it's got wheels. If I can just figure out a way to take passengers, I can make my fortune and retire before I even get into high school."

"Dream on, Jason," Susan snorted.

Just then the driver climbed back on board. He was dripping wet, and not quite as cheerful as he had been when they started out. "Well, folks, I hate to say it, but it doesn't look good."

"What's the problem?" Mr. Rochester asked.

The bus driver shook his head, splattering the teacher with raindrops. "The blasted thing threw a rod," he said.

Nora shook her head, too. "Uh-oh."

"Is that serious?" Tracy asked anxiously.

"On a scale of one to ten it's a nine and a half," Nora told her.

There was confusion in Tracy's blue eyes. "Well, that's good, isn't it?"

"This isn't gymnastics, Tracy," Susan remarked. "It's an engine breakdown."

"Pretty bad one, too," the driver said. "I'm afraid the rod did a lot a lot of damage flying around in there."

"Aargh!" Mitch pretended to look squeamish. "Please, spare us the gory details!"

"Oh, yes!" Tommy joined in, "I have a very weak stomach!"

"Mitch, Tommy." Mr. Rochester looked stern. "That's enough."

Embarrassed, the two boys subsided.

Jennifer stared at the English teacher. Mitch and Tommy weren't the world's greatest comedians, but still, Mr. Rochester usually had a sense of humor, even with them. Now he was acting like a typical teacher.

She glanced at Ms. Spencer, who seemed fascinated with the rain beating against the window. That was the reason, Jennifer thought.

They were so mad at each other they weren't even behaving normally.

"Well, there's one plus, at least," the bus driver said. "We're only a five-minute walk from the heart of downtown Piedmont."

Everybody crowded up to the front windows. Through the rain, they could just make out a few buildings and a traffic light, flashing yellow.

"You're sure that's the heart?" Nora asked.

"That's it," the driver chuckled. "Piedmont's a tiny town. But don't worry, its garage mechanic is a real crackerjack. If anybody can fix this yellow beast, he can." He pulled up the hood of his slicker again. "I'll be back in a jiffy, so everybody sit tight!"

"We don't have much of a choice," Susan commented, as the driver jumped out of the bus and the rest of them went back to their seats. "What do you suppose our chances of seeing *Macbeth* are?"

"Doom-da-doom-doomed," Steve said dramatically.

Fifteen minutes later, the driver came hurrying back with another man, and the two of them checked out the engine together. Without a word to one other, Ms. Spencer and Mr. Rochester put on their raincoats and went outside to join them.

"There's no sense in all of us getting wet," Mr. Rochester called back over his shoulder, "so the rest of you stay here."

Once again, the group moved to the front of the bus and watched the proceedings through the window.

The driver and the mechanic were busy fiddling with the engine; every once in a while, they'd look at each other and shake their heads. But even though they wanted to get going, the students were more interested in what the teachers were doing.

Mitch hopped into the driver's seat. "I'd say it's a pretty even match, folks," he said in the tone of a sports announcer. "On the left, wearing a tan trench coat and carrying a black umbrella, is Cliff Rochester, English teacher. And on the right, also in a tan raincoat but carrying a red umbrella, is art teacher Allison Spencer!"

Tommy and Jason whistled and stamped their feet.

"And there's the bell!" Mitch called out. "They didn't shake hands, but they came out fighting!"

Outside, Ms. Spencer and Mr. Rochester were standing face to face, frowning, and talking at the same time.

"I'd give anything to hear what they're saying," Tracy said.

"Not me," Lucy said. "I'd rather stay in here where it's warm and dry and *friendly*."

"Oh, it looks like a point for Mr. Rochester!" Mitch cried. "Ms. Spencer is walking away!"

Sure enough, the art teacher had turned and walked a few feet away from Mr. Rochester, standing with her back to him.

"It's time for the count," Mitch called. "One . . . two . . . is this going to be a T.K.O.? Four — "

"No!" Tommy had gotten into the spirit of it now. "She's coming back!"

Ms. Spencer had turned and was striding back to Mr. Rochester. Once again, the two teachers faced each other, mouths going a mile a minute, hands gesturing angrily. The mechanic and the driver glanced at them briefly, shrugged at each other, and turned back to the engine.

"It's going to be a close one, folks!" Mitch shouted.

"It looks like it's going to be a long one, too," Nora said. "I think I'll sit back down. I feel like I'm eavesdropping even though I can't hear anything."

Some of the others watched for another minute, but soon everybody straggled back to their seats. They were all strangely quiet.

"I guess it's not so funny after all," Mitch

said finally. "I wish they'd stop fighting."

"What are they fighting about, anyway?" Mia asked.

"Probably something dumb," Andy said. He ran his hand nervously through his bronze stripe and then stepped over Jason's long legs and stood in the aisle in front of Mia. "Like us, huh?"

Mia looked up at him. "You're right," she said with a smile.

"Well, that's one romance that's back on track," Nora said to Jennifer.

Jennifer nodded. "But I have a feeling the other one is like our chances of seeing *Macbeth* — doomed."

Twenty minutes later, the mechanic left, and the driver and two teachers trooped back onto the bus.

"What's the prognosis?" Nora asked them.

Mr. Rochester shook his head. "Pretty bleak, I'm afraid."

Everybody wondered whether he was talking about the romance or the bus.

Ms. Spencer spoke up. "It's not completely bleak," she said, a determined smile on her face. "The bus is beyond repair at the moment, but we'll call for another one. That won't get here in time for us to make tonight's performance, but there's a matinee tomorrow. With a little luck, we should be able to switch our tickets."

"I told you she had both feet on the ground," Denise whispered.

"It's a good thing, too," Tracy whispered back. "Mr. Rochester looks ready to fly through the roof."

Tracy was right. The English teacher's dark eyes were glowing, and not with happiness.

"Gee, that sounds reasonable," the bus driver said, anxious to get everything settled. "That mechanic's my wife's cousin — he'll be more than happy to let you use the phone in his shop."

Mr. Rochester nodded. "Very nice of him. But there's still the matter of where to stay tonight. I don't think my students' parents would be too happy if they spent the night on the bus."

"Who says we have to sleep on the bus?" Ms. Spencer asked.

"Nobody," Mr. Rochester said tightly. "But since we didn't bring sleeping bags, and it's raining anyway, where else do you suggest we put up for the night? *If* we can switch the tickets."

"Oh, gosh, don't worry about that," the bus driver told them eagerly. "Piedmont's small, but it does have a motel. And at this time of year, it's bound to be empty."

"It sounds good to me," Ms. Spencer said. "Does anyone have any objections?"

Nobody did, although Mr. Rochester looked like he objected to the entire world at that moment.

A few minutes later, they were all gathered, bags in hand, in the garage of the Piedmont Auto Repair Shop. Mr. Rochester followed the mechanic into the small adjoining office, and through the window, they could see him grimly pick up the telephone.

Jennifer sneaked a look at Ms. Spencer. She was dripping, like the rest of them, and her wavy, light-brown hair was now a mass of frizz. Her green eyes were very bright, and when she blinked, drops of water fell off her lashes. It could be rain, Jennifer thought. But it might be tears.

"I have an idea," Jennifer said loudly. "This could take a long time and there's no reason for us all to stand around waiting. Just in case we do get to stay, why don't we go make sure the motel has enough vacancies and find someplace to eat?"

"I don't know," Tracy said. "It's still raining out there and — "

"Don't you know humidity is the best thing

in the world for your complexion?" Jennifer said, practically pushing Tracy out the door. "Isn't it, Nora?"

"Sure, if you've got dry skin," Nora said, slightly puzzled. She wasn't sure what Jennifer was up to, but she was willing to go along. "And Tracy, you're always complaining about that."

"No, I'm not," Tracy protested. "My skin's oily."

"It still needs moisture," Jennifer said. "Come on, everybody. Let's go see Piedmont."

"What was that all about?" Nora asked Jennifer as they hurried out the door, after telling Ms. Spencer where they were going.

"I thought Ms. Spencer looked a little upset," Jennifer explained. "Besides, if we leave the two of them together, they might make up."

Nora smiled at her best friend. "I should have guessed," she said.

Once they were outside, they discovered that the rain had stopped completely, which cheered them all. Jason took off down the sidewalk on his skateboard, and the rest of them headed immediately for the drugstore down the street.

On the way, they passed the motel, or BIDE-A-WEE MOTE as the broken sign said, and stopped in front of it.

Not only was its sign broken, but the paint was peeling off the doors, the stucco was chipped and gray, and the gutter was rusted so badly that each room had a huge puddle in front of it.

"I don't think I'd want to bide even a wee in that place," Lucy said.

"It's a disgrace," Denise agreed. "It should be condemned."

"But look on the bright side," Mitch suggested. "It's got cable TV in every room."

"It's probably got bugs in every room, too," Susan said.

"Ooh, yuck!" Tracy cried. "Don't even mention that. I get the creepy-crawlies just thinking about it!"

"Look, for all we know, we might not even have to stay here," Nora said practically. "Let's go get something to eat and go back to the garage. If Mr. Rochester switched our ticket reservations, then we can worry about where to spend the night."

At the drugstore, they bought candy bars and small bags of potato chips — except for Nora, who found two dusty packages of sunflower seeds — and just as they were leaving, Denise discovered a notice on inside of the door.

"We may be in luck," she said. "This town has a B&B."

"A what?" Tracy asked.

"Bed and Breakfast," Denise explained. "It's a very European thing. They're usually private houses where the owners rent rooms and serve home-cooked meals. It's much more personal than a hotel."

" 'Mandeville Manor,' " Jennifer said, reading the notice. " 'Ten spacious rooms with working fireplaces, family-style dining, privacy, comfort, discreet staff.' "

"What's discreet mean?" Mitch asked.

"It means they leave you alone," Susan translated.

"But no TV," he complained.

"I don't know about anybody else," Lucy said, "but I'd rather stay in a manor than a 'mote' any time."

"Moat?" Tracy asked. "It's got a moat, too?"

Susan started to answer, but Nora jumped in first. "I'll explain on the way, Tracy," she said. "Come on, let's go back to the repair shop and find out if we're staying here or not."

When they got back, they found that the mood between Mr. Rochester and Ms. Spencer was as black as ever. But there was some good news — the reservations had been changed, and the trip was still on.

"The next thing to do is call your families and explain the situation," Mr. Rochester said. He gestured to the mechanic. "Mr. Johnson here has been gracious enough to offer us the use of his phone for that, too, so let's get started. Then we'll see about the motel."

"We already saw it," Mia told him. "And it's really bad."

"In the true sense of the word," Steve said.

"But we found another place that sounds perfect," Denise said. "It's called Mandeville Manor and it's — "

"Uh, pardon me." The mechanic looked shy but determined to speak his mind. "You, uh, you don't want to stay at Mandeville."

"Why not?" Denise asked. "It has to be nicer than the motel."

"Oh, it's nicer, all right," Mr. Johnson agreed. "But you still don't want to stay there."

"Why not?" Denise asked again.

"Simple," Mr. Johnson said. "Mandeville Manor is haunted."

Chapter 7

Denise gave a slight shake of her head, and her beautiful blonde hair glimmered in the dingy light of the garage. "Excuse me," she said, "but what did you just say?"

"He said the manor is haunted, my dear," Tommy told her, imitating Count Dracula.

"That's what I thought." Denise turned back to the mechanic. "That *was* what you said, wasn't it?"

Mr. Johnson nodded seriously. "That's what I said, all right. Mandeville Manor is haunted."

"Really weird!" Mia said.

"Really impossible," Nora said.

"I know you don't believe me," the mechanic told them. "But there's just no other explanation for some of the things that go on there, except — "

"Ghosts!" Mitch cackled. "Goblins! Witches!"

"No, just ghosts," Mr. Johnson said, still very serious.

Tracy gasped and put her hand over her mouth. "He means it!" she whispered, her blue eyes wide with fright.

"Wait a minute," Mr. Rochester said to Mr. Johnson, smiling for the first time that day. "You mentioned 'things' that go on there. What 'things' are you talking about?"

Even though it was obvious that he was up against a bunch of skeptics, Mr. Johnson didn't back down. Still looking very grave, he said, "It all started about five years ago, just a few months after Judith Mandeville decided to turn that big place of hers into a boarding house. It seemed like a good idea — she's all alone there since her family died and left it to her, and the upkeep is pretty high."

"Get to the ghosts — ha, ha," urged Tommy-Dracula.

"Well, the first people to stay there were a young couple traveling around on their honeymoon," Mr. Johnson went on. "They registered for three nights, but they only stayed one."

"Here comes the scary part," Steve whispered to Jennifer, squeezing her hand.

"They stopped here on their way out to get some gas," Mr. Johnson said. "And they told me that while they were having dinner, the dishes in the big antique sideboard started rattling like crazy, and then the sideboard itself moved."

"Moved?" Lucy muttered to herself. "Great. Wait'll Jason gets back from wherever he's gone, and hears this!"

"Slid three feet out from the wall and back," Mr. Johnson told her. "Then a couple of pictures started wiggling back and forth."

Nearly everyone still looked skeptical, but Mr. Johnson pushed on. "Others who've stayed there have seen the same thing, and some of them heard voices coming from nowhere, saw lights flickering on and off for no reason. Here's the kicker," he said, "the last people there heard crazy laughter in the middle of the night. So loud and wild it woke them up. It was coming from the room across the hall from theirs, so they figured it was some other guests. They got out of bed, went over and knocked on the door," he said softly. "No answer but the laughing. They knocked again, harder this time, and the door swung open." He paused dramatically.

"And?" Tracy squeaked.

"The room was empty," he finished.

Tracy was obviously a true believer by this time, and even Mia looked a little apprehensive. But nobody else was convinced that there were ghosts at Mandeville Manor.

"There has to be a logical explanation for all of it," Nora spoke up. "Dishes rattling and furniture moving? It could have been an earthquake."

"And the flashing lights," Lucy said. "That was probably just an electrical thing — the weather or the wiring or something."

"Hasn't been an earthquake recorded in these parts for over fifty years," Mr. Johnson said positively. "And Miss Mandeville had an electrician out to check the wiring — it was perfectly sound."

"Then it must have been a storm," Steve said.

"The night was clear and calm," the mechanic told them. "Never saw such a starry night in my life." He smiled grimly. "People who stay there once," he said, "never come back."

"You mean they've all disappeared?!" Tracy cried. She looked ready to dash out the door and go all the way back to Cedar Groves on foot.

"Of course not," Ms. Spencer said briskly. "He means they don't make reservations to stay there again because they've been fooled into believing in ghosts."

"This is almost as good as *Macbeth*," Andy commented.

"But *Macbeth's* not real," Mia said.

"And this isn't, either, Mia," Mr. Rochester said.

Mia nervously fingered one of her spikes. "Yeah, you're right," she admitted. "I *guess*."

"Besides, we just can't stay at that motel," Denise said, who was used to the best accommodations. "It's run-down and dirty and. . . ."

"It's a dump," Mitch finished.

"It really is," Jennifer agreed.

"Well, I don't have any objections to Mandeville Manor," Mr. Rochester said. "That is, if it's not booked up."

"Empty as a tomb," Mr. Johnson said solemnly.

"Did you have to use that word?" Tracy moaned.

"Fear not, my dear," Tommy said, still using his Dracula voice, "I vill protect you!"

The others couldn't help laughing. And Tracy, happy that Tommy was still paying attention to her, finally smiled.

"Good," Ms. Spencer said. "Then we're all agreed."

"Finally," Mr. Rochester said under his breath.

"On that, anyway," Jennifer whispered to Nora.

Denise had taken down the number of

Mandeville Manor, so Ms. Spencer called and made sure there was room, which there was. Frank Hardy, the bus driver, was invited to come with them, but Mr. Johnson persuaded him to stay at his house.

"I'd invite the rest of you," Mr. Johnson said worriedly. "But there's just not room. I sure don't like the idea of you staying out at the manor."

"That's all right, Mr. Johnson," Ms. Spencer assured him. "We'll be just fine."

Mr. Johnson shook his head, but didn't argue. "I've done my job and warned you," he said. "If you still want to stay there, that's your business, I guess."

On that cheerful note, everybody called home to tell their families of the change in plans.

"You won't believe this," Jennifer said to Jeff after she'd reached him and explained everything. "But the place we're staying in tonight is supposed to be haunted."

"Is this connection bad?" Jeff asked. "I thought you said 'haunted.' "

"I did," Jennifer laughed. "But don't worry. And tell Dad not to worry. It's just a rumor and nobody believes it."

"I should hope not," Jeff said. "By the way, it's raining here again — a real thunderstorm this time. You should expect it there in a few hours, so I'm glad you'll have a nice solid roof over your heads."

"Me, too," Jennifer agreed. "I'd better go now. The others have to call. I'll give your regards to Willie and see you tomorrow!"

Jennifer hung up and was walking over to wait with the others when she suddenly noticed that Jason wasn't with them.

"I hope he hasn't gotten homesick again," she said. "He was acting nervous on the bus — he had a funny look on his face."

"Jason Anthony always has a funny look on his face," Susan remarked.

"Maybe a ghost got him," Mitch joked.

"Oh, Mitch, don't say that!" Tracy pleaded.

"This isn't funny, Mitch," Jennifer said. "I can't believe this! In Washington, he went to the bus station. Do you think Piedmont has a bus station?"

"Never mind, there he is," Steve said, pointing toward the door. "In the flesh, too, Tracy."

His red hair flapping wildly, Jason zoomed down the sidewalk toward the waiting group. Screeching to a stop, he kicked the skateboard on one end and flipped it up into his hands. "Hey, I finally did it right," he grinned.

"Where have you been?" Nora demanded. "We were just about ready to go to Mr. Rochester, and with the mood he's in, he probably would have chewed our heads off just for telling him."

"Sorry," Jason said. "I was just coasting around."

"We thought you'd decided to go home," Jennifer told him.

"Nope." Jason looked pleased with himself. "I guess I've conquered my homesickness. But anyway, guess what I found out? I guarantee you're not going to believe this!"

"What?" Nora asked.

Jason grinned again. "This town has a haunted house!"

"We already know that, Jason," Susan said with an even bigger smile. "And that's exactly where we're staying tonight."

The grin disappeared from Jason's face. He'd finally talked himself out of being homesick and now he had to spend the night in a haunted house? A guy really had to be on his toes to survive these field trips!

Mandeville Manor was on the outskirts of Piedmont. But since the town was so small, it didn't take them long to get there. A winding drive led up to the house from the main road; it was bordered by tall maples and dark green shrubs. The rainstorm Jeff had talked about hadn't arrived yet, but everything was dripping and shiny from the first one.

"This is beautiful," Jennifer said, walking with Steve and Nora. Lowering her voice, she went on, "Maybe once we're settled, Mr. Rochester and Ms. Spencer will relax and make up."

Nora's brown eyes crinkled in a smile. "Are you still worrying about those two?"

"Of course I am. They're miserable, can't you tell?"

"Yes," Nora said, "but I don't think there's anything we can do about it." She looked at her friend. "Jen, you can't solve everybody's problems."

"But this is such a stupid one!" Jennifer cried. "They fought over nothing and now they're both just being stubborn."

"You're right about that," Steve agreed. He looked toward Mr. Rochester, who was walking alone in the front of the group, then back at Ms. Spencer, who was bringing up the rear. "It really is a stupid fight. But I don't think either one of them is going to give in first."

"No," Jennifer said, "but if both of them gave in at the same time — " She stopped suddenly, as if she'd just had a brainstorm.

Nora stared at her. "Jen, what are you thinking?"

"I'm not sure yet," Jennifer said, picking her

way around a large puddle. "But I promise I'll tell you when I am."

Mandeville Manor was an enormous, mansionlike stone house, three stories high, with gables and turrets and stained-glass windows. Its front door was of massive dark wood, with brass lamps flanking each side and a gleaming, snarling, brass lion's-head knocker.

"Wow," Mia breathed. "I love that lion's head. It would make a great piece of jewelry."

"This place is gorgeous," Denise said softly. "I never thought I'd see anything like it outside of Europe."

"Can you imagine living in such a big house all by yourself?" Tracy said with a shiver. "I'd go crazy." Suddenly she thought of something. "You don't suppose Miss Mandeville is doing all those things herself, do you? I mean, maybe she's crazy. Maybe she's the one."

Susan looked disgusted. "Tracy, if you'd rather stay in the Bide-A-Wee Motel than this . . . this castle, then *you're* crazy."

"I can't help it," Tracy said. "I just can't stop thinking about what that mechanic told us."

While Susan tried to convince Tracy that there were no ghosts in the house, Mr. Rochester walked up to the front door and rattled the knocker. In the meantime, Mitch nudged

Tommy and the two of them began creeping up behind Tracy.

"Tracy!" Mitch said, in what he thought was a ghostly voice. "Tracy Douglas, your time has come!"

Tracy started to turn, but before she did, Tommy leaped behind her and put his hands over her eyes. "It's the ghost!" he shrieked. "Gotcha!"

Even though she knew who it was, Tracy let out a piercing scream.

At that moment, the front door of Mandeville Manor swung open with a loud, slow, rasping creak that was straight out of a horror movie.

Chapter 8

In the doorway stood a small, plump woman about seventy-five years old. Her hair was snowy white, her eyes were bright blue and smiling, and her face was soft and round and beaming with friendliness.

"Welcome," she said in a clear, sweet voice. "You must be the group from Cedar Groves."

"Your worries are over, Tracy," Susan whispered. "If she's a ghost, she's Casper's grandmother."

"I'm Judith Mandeville," the woman said. "Come in, come in! I'm sure you're tired and ready to get out of those wet raincoats and relax."

The entrance hall was almost as big as Jennifer's bedroom, with a high ceiling, old-fashioned coatracks, and a wide-plank oak floor that shone like glass. As the group filed past Miss Mandeville, she smiled pleasantly at everyone, asking a few questions about how they were feeling and which play they were going to see. She was the perfect hostess — warm and welcoming but not pushy with her friendliness.

Jason was the last one in, and as he passed her, she smiled and then reached into the deep pocket of her long cardigan sweater. Out came a can of 4-in-1 Oil, which she proceeded to apply to the hinges of the front door.

"It seems like I did this just yesterday," she said. "I suppose it's time for new hinges."

Jason felt better immediately. Anybody who carried an oil can in her sweater pocket was all right. He was eyeing the oil hopefully when Nora nudged him.

"Don't even think about it, Jason," she told him. "That skateboard would ruin these floors."

Jason was insulted. "Do I look like the kind of guy who'd skateboard in somebody's house?"

"Jason," Susan said, "you *are* the kind of guy who'd skateboard in somebody's house."

"I'm crushed to be so misunderstood," Jason claimed, dramatically clutching his chest. "I was merely thinking of borrowing the oil so that if I decide to go outside, my board will be in tip-top shape."

Straightening up, Miss Mandeville held out the oil can to him. "Be my guest," she smiled.

"I know what it's like to try to keep things in shape."

Jason thanked her and then, tucking the oil in his back pocket, he gave Nora and Susan a triumphant grin.

"Now then," Miss Mandeville said to everyone, "just leave your rain gear here in the hall, and I'll show you the bedrooms. Dinner is usually at six o'clock, but since it's so late already, I've delayed it an hour to give you time to wash and change, if you like."

The bedrooms were on the second and third floors of the house, and as they trooped up the wide carpeted staircase, Miss Mandeville gave them a brief history of the place.

"Mandeville Manor was built in the mid-nineteenth century by my grandfather," she said. "When my mother married, she and my father came back here to live. I was born here and so was my brother."

"Does your brother help run the place?" Steve asked.

"No." Miss Mandeville's smile faded for a second. "James is in Europe." Then her cheerfulness returned as she threw open one of the bedroom doors. "Here we are — this is one of my favorite rooms."

"I can see why," Jennifer said admiringly. "It's beautiful."

It was a large room, with several small rugs making cheerful splashes of color on the gleaming wood floor. The bed was an old-fashioned four-poster with an intricately patterned multicolored quilt on it, and there was a fire blazing in the promised fireplace, giving the whole room a rosy glow.

Every room was different — some had carpeting, some had two double beds — for families, Miss Mandeville explained — some had closets while others had antique armoires, but all of them were warm and inviting. Four of the ten bedrooms weren't available — not because of guests, she explained — but because they were being painted.

"I'll leave it to you to divide yourselves up," she said, when they'd finished touring the third floor. "Each room has a phone that connects to my rooms downstairs, so you can call if you need anything, until nine-thirty at night. And anytime if there's an emergency, of course." She smiled and folded her hands in front of her. "I do think you'll find all the comforts of home here."

"Whose home?" Mitch quipped, "yours or the ghost's?"

Tommy snickered, but Mr. Rochester gave both boys a stern look. "Not a good joke, you two."

"Oh, it's all right," Miss Mandeville said with a sigh. "Believe me, I've heard every ghost joke that was ever made."

"It's just that we heard some stories in town," Jennifer said, feeling like they owed Miss Mandeville an explanation. "The mechanic at the repair shop was so serious about it, I guess it kind of stuck in some of our minds."

"Some of our *tiny* minds," Susan added, giving Tommy and Mitch a look.

"It sticks in lot of people's minds, unfortunately," Miss Mandeville said. "Which is very bad for business, as you can imagine. But," she went on brightly, "you're all young and modern, and I know you don't believe a lot of foolish talk." She patted her hair and smiled at Tommy and Mitch, who looked a little ashamed of themselves. "Now, dinner's in an hour, and it'll be a hearty one. I know how young people are — always hungry."

"Miss Mandeville is really nice, isn't she?" Jennifer asked later. She rummaged around in her duffel bag and pulled out her hairbrush. "You can tell this house means a lot to her. I felt so bad when Mitch cracked that stupid joke about the ghost."

"She is nice," Tracy agreed, plugging in her curling iron. "But you notice she didn't explain away all those creepy things that happened here."

Nora was emptying her overnight case, carefully shaking out the clothes and hanging them up in the big armoire. "Just because she can't explain them doesn't mean there isn't an explanation, Tracy."

The three of them were in what Miss Mandeville called the blue bedroom. It had a double and a single bed, both with blue comforters; pale blue curtains at the windows; and blue-and-white tiles around the fireplace. Lucy, Mia, Susan, and Denise were in a room across the hall, and Ms. Spencer was two doors down. The boys and Mr. Rochester were staying on the third floor. In half an hour, they would all be going downstairs for the big dinner Miss Mandeville had promised them.

"I know there's an explanation," Tracy said now, winding a thick strand of blonde hair up in the curling iron. "I'd just like to know what it is, that's all. I guess I really don't believe in ghosts, but still, strange things did happen here."

"Cheer up, Tracy," Nora told her. "Remember what Tommy said — he'll protect you."

"Right," Jennifer agreed with a laugh. "If a ghost comes along, Tommy will slay it with his comb!"

"No he won't," Nora giggled. "He wouldn't dare use his comb — what if his hair got messed up? His image would be ruined. I know!" she said, grinning at Jennifer. "We can throw Jeff's Coconolas at it!"

"Or at Tommy!" Jennifer laughed.

While Jennifer and Nora joked, Tracy finished her hair and then stood in front of the big oval mirror over the dressing table and started putting on some soft blue eye shadow.

Finishing with the eye shadow, Tracy carefully applied eyeliner along her lashline with a new pencil. It was called Dusky Mink, and she'd bought it just for the trip. Of course, she'd planned to wear it to dinner at the hotel, not here in this spooky house. She didn't care how big and beautiful Mandeville Manor was, it was still a spooky place. A hotel would be busy and bustling with people; this place was so quiet and still — and isolated — it really gave her the creeps.

At that moment, there was a loud knock at the door. Tracy squealed and jumped and drew a bold line of Dusky Mink straight up over her eyebrow and onto her forehead.

"Nice makeup job," Susan remarked, coming in the room with Mia, Denise, and Lucy.

Tracy sighed and reached for a makeup-remover pad. Susan always seemed to be around when things like this happened.

"Actually, it's kind of interesting," Mia said, peering at Tracy's face. "If you drew a matching one on the other side, they'd look like two flashes of lightning."

"Isn't this house great?" Denise asked, inspecting one of the bedside lamps. She'd changed into a pair of pants and a top in a deep plum color, and the oversized top was gathered around the waist with a wide pink leather belt. "You know, I think this is Tiffany."

"Oh, I love her songs," Tracy said, thinking Denise was talking about a singer who was popular at the moment.

"Not me," Mia said. She'd dressed for dinner, too. Gone were the tight studded jeans, and in their place were a pair of equally tight gray stirrup pants, topped by a shiny silver motorcycle jacket with padded shoulders. "She's so pop."

"Denise was talking about the lamp," Susan said dryly.

"You mean Tiffany has one like it?" Tracy asked.

Lucy laughed, shaking her head at the confusion. "Let's save the explanations for later," she said. "Am I the only one around here who's starving?"

"No, I am, too," Jennifer agreed. "I wonder what they'll serve?"

"Whatever it is, I hope there's a lot of it," Lucy said, patting her flat stomach. "I plan to keep them going back to the kitchen for seconds, maybe even thirds."

" 'They?' " Tracy asked. "I haven't seen any 'they.' The only person I've seen is Miss Mandeville." She glanced around the room nervously and lowered her voice. "That's another peculiar thing about this house, in case nobody else noticed."

"The ad said the staff was discreet," Denise reminded her.

"Discreet is fine," Tracy said. "But invisible is just plain weird."

Susan clicked her tongue. "Honestly, Tracy. Are you going to keep that up the whole time we're here? Even Mia's not scared anymore."

Mia nodded, her blue feather earrings brushing her silver shoulders. "I've been trying to see if I could feel any negative vibrations in this house," she said. "It's real easy, once you get the hang of it."

Everyone was listening to Mia except Tracy, who had heard something.

"All you have to do," Mia went on, "is kind of put everything out of your mind — just empty it, like you're cleaning out the refrigerator."

"That should be easy for Tracy," Susan commented under her breath. "Her mind *is* an empty refrigerator."

But Tracy didn't hear the insult. She was staring at the ceiling.

"Then," Mia said, "you wait and see what comes in. That's the hard part . . ."

"Look," Tracy whispered.

". . . because sometimes my mind just wanders and. . . ."

"Look!" Tracy cried, pointing to the ceiling.

Everyone looked. In the center of the ceiling was a hanging bronze light fixture with ten candle-shaped bulbs in it. It was swaying back and forth, and as they watched the bulbs began to flicker and the fixture started to swing wildly over their heads.

Without taking her eyes off of it, Tracy croaked, "What kind of vibrations do you get from that, Mia?"

Chapter 9

On the third floor, directly above the blue room, Mitch and Tommy grinned at each other as they jumped up and down in the middle of the floor. They'd seen the girls' room earlier, and the hanging light fixture was too tempting to pass up.

"One more good jump and then we stop," Tommy said. "Let them think it's over. Once they calm down, we'll start up again." He and Mitch jumped, landing heavily.

"Okay, that's enough," Tommy told him. "Now we act casual. If they don't come running in a few minutes, we'll do it again."

Jason, who hadn't been jumping, watched as the other two leaped onto their beds and stretched out with their copies of *Macbeth*. Their plan was to scare the girls and then play the heroes and try to find out what was making the light fixture shake. That way, they'd get the girls running to them for protection.

Jason thought about how Mitch and Tommy always had girls trailing after them, and now he was beginning to understand why. They didn't just sit around waiting for something to happen — they made it happen. If they could do it, why couldn't he?

Jason leaped off his bed and crossed to the center of the floor. If it worked for Mitch and Tommy, it just might work for him. He lifted one of his long legs until his knee almost touched his chin, and he was just about ready to stomp down when the door flew open.

Nora was in the doorway, and behind her were all the rest of the girls.

"I knew it!" Nora cried. "Tracy, come in and see your ghost."

Tracy edged her way into the room and stared at Jason, who stood as if frozen, his knee nearly grazing his chin. "Jason Anthony!" she said. "I should have guessed!"

Slowly, Jason lowered his foot, grinning sheepishly. Mitch and Tommy peered innocently over the tops of their books. "Guessed what?" Mitch asked.

"Wait a minute," Denise said suspiciously. "What are the two of you reading?"

The boys lifted their books so she could see

the covers. "Just boning up on the Bard of Avon," Tommy said, hoping to impress her.

But Denise wasn't impressed. Turning to the others, she said, "They were in on it, too."

"Absolutely," agreed Lucy.

"In fact," Nora said, "it was probably their idea."

Mia shook her head. "And they were going to let poor Jason take all the blame for it," she said scornfully.

"Hey, we wouldn't do that," Mitch said, winking at Jason.

"Gotcha!" Jennifer said. "Nice try, but we don't scare that easily."

Laughing, the girls turned and walked back out the door. Once they were in the hall, Tracy asked, "How did you know Mitch and Tommy were part of it? After all, they were just lying there reading."

"Tracy," Nora said, still laughing, "when you see those two reading Shakespeare without anybody telling them to, you can bet they're trying to hide something!"

With the "Shaking Chandelier Ghost" laid to rest, everyone finally went downstairs for dinner. The dining room, which they hadn't seen earlier, was incredible. Huge and wood-paneled, half of it was taken up by an enormous, baronial-like table with intricately carved, high-backed chairs. The other half of the room had bookshelves reaching to the ceiling, a huge fireplace, and deep leather armchairs. Oriental rugs were under the table and in front of the fireplace, and vases of flowers added touches of fresh color.

Steve gave a low whistle. "These field trips are getting better and better."

"Too bad there's not a stereo in here," Andy said. "I'll bet the acoustics are fantastic."

"I've never seen a dining room like this before," Jason said, slightly awed.

"Neither have I," Susan agreed. "But it wouldn't take me long to get used to it." She laughed. "Actually, it would. I feel pretty shabby wearing pants and a sweater in this place. If I lived here, I'd have to get myself a long silk dress just to eat dinner in."

"Yes, my dear," Tommy said in a haughty voice, peering at her through an imaginary monocle. "We are all definitely underdressed, tut, tut! I told my valet to pack my tux, but the varlet forgot."

Susan laughed again. It was amazing, but sometimes Tommy actually showed signs of being human. And he was awfully cute, although she'd never let him — or Tracy — hear her say it. If he acted like this more often, she'd have a lot of trouble not liking him.

"Look at all this," Jennifer said, standing in front of the massive sideboard. On it were several covered chafing dishes. Let's see what we're having." She lifted one of the silver lids.

"Empty," Mitch said, peering over her shoulder and looking disappointed.

Tracy was staring up at the glass-doored shelves over the sideboard. "This is it," she whispered. "This is the piece of furniture Mr. Johnson was talking about. The one that moved!"

"Those people must have been imagining things," Lucy told her. "That sideboard weighs a ton."

"It looks like it weighs a ton, you mean," Mitch corrected her. He went to the end of the sideboard, put his hands underneath and tried to lift it. All he got for his effort was a red face. "You're right," he panted, "it weighs a ton."

"Tracy," Nora said, "if we all try to lift this thing and can't, will that put your mind at ease?"

Before Tracy had a chance to answer, everybody was gathered around the sideboard.

"On the count of three," Mitch directed. "One . . . two . . . three, heave!"

Everybody heaved, but nothing budged.

"What's going on?" a voice said.

They turned to see Mr. Rochester in the doorway, a frown on his handsome face. Without waiting for an answer, he stepped into the room and said, "This isn't the kind of behavior I expected. We happen to be guests in this house. Just because we're paying guests doesn't mean you have the right to turn this place into an amusement park."

The students stared at him silently, embarrassed and confused. Mr. Rochester didn't talk to them like this. He was usually so understanding and didn't care if they sometimes acted like idiots. He usually had a sense of humor. Now he looked like he was on his way to a funeral.

"They were conducting an experiment," Ms. Spencer said. She was standing in the doorway now. Her hair was piled on top of her head, and she wore diamond drop earrings. She looked extremely elegant in dark red silk pants and matching top. She walked into the room, passed Mr. Rochester, and smiled at everyone but him. "What was the result?" she asked.

The boys were still staring at her, openmouthed, so Nora decided to answer. "We couldn't budge it," she said. "It had to be an earthquake."

Ms. Spencer laughed. "Well, I can't blame you for trying. I probably would have done the same thing." Still not glancing at Mr. Rochester, she walked to the head of the dining table and pulled out the chair. "I saw Miss Mandeville as I came in, and I think she's just about ready to serve dinner. Why don't we all sit down? I think we deserve a good meal after that bus ride, don't you?"

As the delicious dinner was served, Tracy finally got to see the rest of the staff, which consisted of one man, as plump as Miss Mandeville and just as friendly. He filled their water glasses and made sure the serving dishes on the sideboard were never empty.

Tracy whispered to Susan, "I bet he goes home after he's finished. And we're going to be stuck here alone."

"What do you mean, alone?" Lucy teased. "You heard Tommy — he'll protect you."

"Ha," Tracy said. She was still slightly annoyed that Mitch and Tommy had tried to scare them earlier. "Tommy's just a boy. I'd feel much safer with a man. But a whole gang of ghosts could appear right now, and I don't think Mr. Rochester would even notice."

Tracy was right. Mr. Rochester concentrated totally on his food.

Jennifer watched the teachers during the meal. Mr. Rochester was silent and stony-faced; Ms. Spencer was bright and chatty. But as far as Jennifer was concerned, both of them were miserable. Every once in a while, she'd catch them looking at each other. They'd look away real fast, of course, but Jennifer knew that if they really hated each other, they wouldn't even bother to look. Besides, Ms. Spencer was still wearing her engagement ring. That had to mean something.

The romance wasn't doomed yet, Jennifer thought. Maybe all it needed was a little push to get it going in the right direction again.

"Now then," Miss Mandeville said, as she stacked the dessert plates on a tray. "I'll leave the fruit and cheese on the sideboard, in case anyone wants to nibble. This room is open until ten, so feel free to stay down here and talk or read until then." She picked up the tray and smiled as she headed out of the room. "Breakfast is at eight-thirty, so if I don't see you before then, I hope you have a restful night."

Everyone thanked her for the great meal, and as soon as she was gone, Mr. Rochester stood up. "I'll say good-night now," he told them. "I brought some papers with me to grade. See you in the morning."

After he left the room, Ms. Spencer glanced at her watch, sipped some coffee, and glanced at her watch again.

"She's giving him enough time to get up to his room before she leaves," Jennifer whispered to Nora, as they both went over to the sideboard. "She doesn't want to take any chances on running into him."

"I know, it's really obvious," Nora said. She studied the bowl of fruit and took a pear. "It's going to make it pretty hard for them to get back together if they won't even stay in the same room with each other."

"Like I said, I've been thinking about that," Jennifer reminded her, biting into an apple.

"I know," Nora grinned.

Jennifer laughed. She could always trust Nora to know what she was feeling. "Well, unfortunately, I didn't come up with the perfect solution," she said. "And time's running out. If we don't do something fast, the two of them might actually call off their engagement."

"We?" Nora asked. "You mean *I'm* going to be in on this, too, whatever it is?"

"We're *all* going to be in on it," Jennifer said, gesturing toward the rest of the group. "This is the perfect room for a meeting and I think it's about time we had one, don't you?"

"I guess so." Nora had her doubts about whether they could do anything to get the two teachers back together again, but Jennifer was positive they could, and she wasn't about to let Jennifer down. "Okay," she said, "let's have a meeting."

"Great! I knew I could count on you," Jennifer said. "By the way," she went on, "I thought we'd call this one 'Operation Lovesave'!"

Chapter 10

Once Ms. Spencer had left, and they felt sure she wasn't coming back, Jennifer and Nora spread the word for everyone to gather over by the fireplace.

Jason scooped up a handful of little mints from a cut-glass dish and popped them all into his mouth. "What could be finer than an after-dinner mint?"

"Nothing, except you're not supposed to scarf them down like M&M's," Susan remarked, shaking her head. "Jason, you're hopeless."

"That's exactly what I want to talk about," Jennifer said, as everyone moved toward the fireplace.

"Jason's hopeless condition?" Susan asked. "Sorry, Jennifer, but it's a lost cause."

Grinning, Jason took some more mints and

began tossing them in the air, trying to catch them with his mouth.

"See what I mean?" Susan added.

"I don't want to talk about Jason at all," Jennifer said. She glanced toward the door and lowered her voice, just in case. "I want to talk about Mr. Rochester and Ms. Spencer."

"Now there's a hopeless condition," Tommy observed.

"Right," Mitch agreed, lounging comfortably in one of the big leather chairs. "It looks like the big romance is fading fast."

Jennifer sighed. Didn't those two ever see anything but the obvious? "It *looks* like it's fading," she said, "but I don't think either one of them really wants it to fade. I think they're both miserable."

"Gee, Ms. Spencer was talking up a storm at dinner," Jason said. "She didn't look miserable to me."

"But Jason," Denise argued, "don't you ever try to hide your feelings?"

"Me?" Jason looked surprised. Then he remembered what he'd decided on the bus. "Sure, sometimes."

"And if you didn't want somebody to know how you felt," Denise went on, sounding like an extremely patient teacher with an extremely slow student, "what would you do?"

"Well. . . ." Jason stopped and thought about it, his reddish eyebrows wrinkling. "I'd pretend to be feeling something else. Oh, I get it," he said. "You think that's what Ms. Spencer was doing."

"The light dawns," Susan remarked.

"Thanks, Denise," Jennifer said gratefully. "Anyway," she went on, "if they're both miserable, and they're both too stubborn to do anything about it, then I think it's about time *we* did something about it."

Susan was shaking her head. Put Jennifer down in the middle of a desert, and she'd find a cause to support. "This isn't like saving the whales, you know," she said. "You can't just go around sticking your nose into other people's business. If they want to be mad, they have a right to be mad."

"But they don't want to be mad," Lucy said. "That's what Jennifer means."

"It's very simple," Nora said, coming to Jennifer's rescue. "Jen thinks we ought to figure out a way to get Ms. Spencer and Mr. Rochester back together again. I'm ready to help come up with some ideas. What about everybody else?"

"Sort of play matchmakers, you mean?" Mia asked.

"Re-matchmakers," Jennifer said.

"It's worth a try, I guess," Steve said, smiling at Jennifer. "What is there to lose?"

"Mr. Rochester's temper," Jason commented.

"He's already lost that," Lucy told him.

"Well, I think it's a great idea," Tracy said. "Except I can't think of anything to do."

"I've got it. How about if we lock them in the same room together," Mitch suggested, "and not let them out until they either make up or beat each other up?"

"Music," Andy said. "They'd hear some music, they'd start dancing, pretty soon they'd forget everything else."

"Wow, that's right," Mia agreed. "And I've got my recorder. If we could get them together, I could put on a tape and. . . ."

"And they'd go crazy," Lucy laughed. "Sorry, Mia. But punk isn't most people's idea of romantic music."

"How about apology notes?" Tracy suggested. She'd finally caught on to the spirit of the plan. "They each write a note saying 'I'm sorry.' "

"How are you going to get them to do that?" Susan sneered. "Hold a gun to their heads?"

"*They* don't do it," Tracy said, as if it should be obvious even to a total idiot. "Somebody does it *for* them."

Susan didn't say anything, and Tracy smiled, very pleased with herself. For once, she'd made Susan look like the airhead.

"I like the locked-room idea better," Mitch said. "Picture it — they're stuck, they can't get out, Ms. Spencer says, 'Oh, Cliffie, Cliffie, what are we going to do?!' " He laughed at his imitation of the helpless female.

"Yeah," Tommy said, "then he puts his arm around her and says . . ." Tommy deepened his voice and squared his jaw. " '. . . Don't worry, Allie, I'll get us out of here. You can always count on me!' "

The girls groaned and booed. "That sounds like a fifty-year-old movie," Denise said scornfully. "But I have to admit, the idea of getting them in the same room — alone — isn't bad."

"With some music," Mia added.

"After they get the apology notes," Tracy said.

"We can't do them *all*," Jennifer laughed. Then she changed her mind. "Wait a minute, why not? We don't know what's going to work, anyway. So why not hit them with everything?"

After some more discussion, it was decided — Tracy would write the notes, Mia would go through the tapes she'd brought and see if she could find something that wasn't too outrageously punk, and the boys volunteered to figure out a way to get the two teachers down to the dining room.

"Are you sure we can trust those guys to come up with something subtle enough?" Lucy asked as she and the rest of the girls left the dining room. "After all, that's the most important part of the plan they're talking about in there."

"Somehow, I don't think that's what they're talking about right now," Nora said with a knowing look. "In fact, I bet they're not even thinking about Mr. Rochester and Ms. Spencer yet. They're thinking about us."

"Oh, I hope so," Tracy said.

"No, not like that," Nora told her. Tracy's boy-craziness really got in the way of her reasoning powers sometimes. "They're trying to figure out another way to scare us," she said.

"But they already tried that," Tracy said.

"Tried and failed," Denise reminded her. "And they're just juvenile enough to try again."

Tracy looked unbelieving, so Nora pulled her over to the dining room door, which was open just a crack. "Listen," she hissed.

Tracy listened, her blue eyes getting wide and indignant. Nora listened, too, holding her hand over her mouth to keep from laughing out loud.

"It's a very simple plan," she reported, when she and Tracy tiptoed back to the others who were waiting halfway up the staircase.

"Simple or simple-minded?" Susan asked.

"Both." Nora ran her fingers through her short brown hair and grinned. "And I say we turn the tables on them."

Fifteen minutes later, there was a frantic knock on the bedroom door, and Tracy went to answer it. Tommy was standing in the hall, looking convincingly scared.

"Down in the dining room!" he said breathlessly. "Something really weird happened!"

"Maybe we should call Ms. Spencer and Mr. Rochester," Nora suggested, coming to the door.

"No, don't do that!" Tommy said quickly.

Jennifer looked innocently surprised. "Why not?"

"Well. . . ." Tommy thought fast. "There's no sense in scaring them, too. Just come on and see!"

Soon, all the girls were following Tommy downstairs. As planned, Lucy lagged behind, but Tommy was so busy pretending to be terrified that he didn't notice.

"You're not going to believe this," he kept saying. "You're just not going to believe it!"

"He's right," Mia whispered, trying not to giggle.

"Ssh," Nora warned. "We don't want to give ourselves away."

When they entered the dining room, they found that it was almost completely dark. All the lights were off, the curtains were drawn, and the fire had died to its last few embers. The boys were shadowy figures in the dimness.

"I don't see how we're supposed to see anything," complained Susan as only Susan could. "Why don't you turn on the lights, for crying out loud?"

She reached for the light switch, but Tommy stopped her. "Don't do that," he said, blocking her. "I have a feeling it's only going to happen in the dark."

"What's going to happen in the dark?" Denise asked, a slight quiver in her voice.

If Tommy had really been listening, he would have realized that the cool Denise Hendrix would never allow her voice to quiver. But he was too busy enjoying his role to notice.

"You'll see," he promised. "Just move over by the fireplace, away from the dining room table."

The girls did as they were told, trying to

keep their faces straight and their eyes off the dining room table, which was now covered with a tablecloth that reached to the floor.

Out of the corner of her eye, Nora saw three of the shadows move toward the table. She counted to ten.

"No matter what happens, try not to scream. It's scary, but I'm pretty sure it's harmless," Tommy said. He took a deep breath. "Now, watch the table!"

Nora nudged Tracy. "Act your heart out," she whispered.

"Oh, my gosh!" Tracy cried. "What's that?!"

"What? Where?" Tommy asked.

"There!" Tracy cried, pointing to the floor over by the windows.

"I see it, too!" Nora said. "Look! It's much too big to be a mouse. I hate to say it, but I think it's a rat!"

"Two rats!" Mia chimed in.

"Rats!" Tommy cried. "You're supposed to be watching the table."

"Watch it?" Tracy shrieked. "I'm going to get on it!" She rushed to the table and climbed on top of it.

"I'm not proud," Jennifer said, dashing to the table after her. "Mice don't bother me, but rats?"

"They bite," Susan said, joining the other

two girls on the tabletop. "And they carry diseases!"

"There are no rats in here. Come on, get off the table," Tommy pleaded.

The girls sat fast. "If anything supernatural is going to happen, it can happen with us on the table," Jennifer told him.

"Okay, but don't say I didn't warn you," Tommy said. "Now watch what happens."

Nothing happened.

"I said, watch what happens," Tommy repeated loudly.

This time, grunts and groans could be heard coming from under the table.

"It's the rats," Jennifer said.

"It's not rats!" Tommy sounded exasperated.

"Oh, yes it is!" Tracy said.

Climbing down off the table, the girls pulled the cloth off. Underneath were Steve, Mitch, and Andy, the unsuccessful ghosts who had tried to lift and shake the table on their backs.

"See?" Susan said triumphantly. "Rats!"

"Honestly," Jennifer said, shaking her head. "Did you really think we'd fall for that?"

"You would have if it hadn't been for whatever Tracy saw by the window," Mitch said, crawling out from under the table.

"I didn't see anything by the window," Tracy told him gleefully.

"And even if we had, we wouldn't have jumped on the table," Susan said. "That's comic-book stuff. Just like your little trick."

Meanwhile, Mia, Nora, and Denise, who hadn't been on the table, were edging their way to the dining room door. Nora pulled it open, and then the three of them fell back into the room, pretending to gasp in fear.

Jason saw it first. He pointed toward the door, his mouth moving soundlessly. Finally he managed to whisper, "Look!"

The others stopped joking with each other and looked toward the door. Standing there, backlit by the dim hall light, was a tall figure draped in black from head to toe. Its hands, which were the only things that showed, had silvery streaks on them, like iridescent bones.

"It's . . . it's . . ." Jason stammered.

"It's me!" Lucy cried, whipping off the black cloth and holding out her hands. "Me and some of Mia's frosted silver hair color!"

The boys looked sheepish. The girls hooted with laughter and headed for the door.

"Gotcha again!" Jennifer called back over her shoulder.

Chapter 11

"That was fun!" Jennifer said when they'd gone back to their room. "Did you see the look on Jason's face? He's pale anyway, but this time he was downright ghostly!" She sat cross-legged on the big bed and started brushing her hair.

"It served him right," Tracy said indignantly, starting to take off her makeup. "Playing such a mean trick."

"It wasn't just Jason, Tracy," Nora reminded her. She took her red Dr. Denton's from the closet and tossed them on the bed. "It was all of them, remember? Including cosmically cute Tommy Ryder."

"I know." Tracy sighed and then brightened up. "It was his idea, though. That shows he's not as stupid as you're always saying."

"Wrong guy," Jennifer said. "It's Mitch who's not too bright."

"Not too strong, either," Nora laughed. "He and Steve and Andy were trying so hard to lift that table, I was afraid they'd pass out."

Tracy giggled. "Then you could have given them mouth-to-mouth."

Nora hooted. "Tracy, you've got a one-track mind."

"But it's such a fun track," Tracy said, giggling again.

Jennifer scooted off the bed, rummaged in her duffel bag and pulled out a pad and pencil. "Here," she said, handing them to Tracy. "First things first. Write those notes and then you can dream about boys."

"Oh, don't worry, I can do both," Tracy assured her.

"Keep it short," Nora said, stepping into her pajamas and closing the snaps. "You don't know what they'd say if they were really writing an apology note."

"Okay." Tracy thought a second. "How about, 'Cliff, darling. I'm so very sorry. I've been an idiot. Please, please forgive me.' "

Jen and Nora rolled their eyes. "Well, it's short," Jennifer said, trying to be tactful. "But I don't think Ms. Spencer would ever call herself an idiot."

"She's not the kind to beg for forgiveness, either," Nora added. "And we don't know if she calls him 'darling.' "

Tracy chewed the pencil and thought some more. "Okay," she said after a few minutes. " 'Dear Cliff, I'm very sorry about everything.' " She shook her head. "That seems too short."

"I have it," Jennifer said, pulling on her furry yellow pajamas. "The guys were so busy trying to scare us, they forgot to figure out a way to get them downstairs together. So after the first part, say 'Meet me in the dining room and let's talk.' "

"Can't I at least say 'please meet me in the dining room'?" Tracy asked. "It sounds like an order without it, and Mr. Rochester isn't in any mood to take orders."

"When you're right, you're right," Nora agreed. "Put in the 'please.' "

"Hold it," Jennifer said, coming over to stand behind Tracy at the dressing table. "We forgot something — we don't know Ms. Spencer's handwriting."

"Ooh, and Mr. Rochester's looks like squiggly little chicken scratches," Tracy said. "I don't think I could do it."

Nora came up with the solution. "Just print

them," she said. "You know how Mr. Rochester's always telling us to read for the content? We'll just have to hope they're both so interested in the content, they won't notice the handwriting."

Finally, it was done, and by a vote of two to one, Tracy was elected to deliver the notes.

"It was your idea," Nora reminded her. "Don't you want to be the one to see it through?"

"Besides," Jennifer added, "you're not in your p.j.'s yet."

"Well, all right," Tracy said. "But if I get caught, I expect you to stand by me."

"Of course we will," Nora teased. "We'll be by your side all the way to the firing squad."

"Very funny," Tracy said. Taking a deep breath, she opened the door of the room, peeked up and down the hall, and then stepped out, closing the door softly behind her.

Inside, Jennifer leaned against the closed door and gave Nora a thumbs-up signal. "Operation Lovesave, Phase One, is now under way!"

In the hallway, Tracy took another look around. Empty. Quiet. Spooky. Why did I ever let them talk me into this? she thought. Jennifer should be delivering these notes — this whole Save the Romance thing was her idea in the first place.

Still, it would be nice if it worked. Tracy wasn't convinced that Ms. Spencer was exactly the right person for the incredibly divine Mr. Rochester, but if *he* was convinced, then she'd just have to accept it. And do her part.

Taking another deep breath, she tiptoed down the hall to the stairs, having decided to deliver Mr. Rochester's note first. He seemed madder than Ms. Spencer, so it would probably take him longer to swallow his pride and go downstairs.

Still on tiptoes, Tracy climbed the stairs to the third floor, testing every step to make sure it didn't creak. At this rate, she thought, it'll be midnight before I get there.

Finally, though, she made it. There were three lights in the hall ceiling, both dim. But not flickering, thank goodness. She stopped and listened. Silence. Not even a murmur from behind the closed doors.

The boys had said that Mr. Rochester's room was at the end of the hall on the left, so Tracy began inching her way down there, barely breathing. By the time she got there, she'd forgotten which note was which. And the envelopes were sealed.

Think, Tracy, think! she told herself. If you goof up, Susan will never let you or anybody else forget it.

She had a note in each hand. The one in the right was — of course! Right for Rochester! Now all she had to do was slip it under the door as quietly as possible. Then she could run.

Tracy was just starting to bend down in front of Mr. Rochester's door when she heard a noise, a high-pitched whining noise like a cat getting ready to fight.

Afterward, Tracy was proud of herself — she didn't scream. She did gasp, though, and she was so frightened that she crushed both envelopes in her hands and backed away so quickly that she slammed up against the wall behind her.

"Hi, Trace," Jason said, sounding extremely casual as he pulled his squeaky bedroom door shut behind him.

"Jason Anthony!" Tracy hissed, hurrying down the hall to him. "If this is your idea of another trick, I'm going to personally break your skateboard in half — over your head!"

"What trick?" Jason looked sincerely confused. "I was just going to brush my teeth." He held up a red toothbrush with mangled bristles and a tube of toothpaste that was rolled up to its very tip. "The accommodations up here are more primitive than those on your floor, madam. We have to share a bathroom, while your rooms have private ones."

Tracy whispered furiously, "All right, maybe it wasn't a trick. But you scared me half to death, and look!" She held up the crumpled notes. "Now I have to write them all over again."

"Well, I'm sorry, Tracy," Jason said. "Could I help it if — " He stopped, his head cocked to one side. "Listen. . . . Do you hear that?"

Tracy was trying to smooth out the envelopes, hoping the notes could be salvaged. The only thing she heard was the crinkling of the paper.

"Ssh," Jason whispered. "Listen."

The notes were beyond saving anyway. With a sigh, Tracy stopped and listened. "I don't hear a thing," she said, starting for the stairs.

"Wait a minute, there it is again!"

This time, Tracy heard it, too. "It's music," she whispered.

"Yeah. Weird music." Jason's face was so pale, his freckles looked as if they'd been painted on.

The music was tinny, like something from an old-fashioned movie, and it seemed to be coming from far away.

"Remember what that mechanic said?" Jason whispered. "Do you think . . . ?"

By now, Tracy had thought of the same thing. She wished it was Tommy out here with her instead of Jason Anthony. It would have been much more romantic to be terrified with Tommy Ryder.

Then she remembered — Tommy had been behind those other tricks. Well, as much as she liked Tommy, she wasn't going to fall for another one. She looked closely at Jason. He was chewing his bottom lip. Probably trying to keep from laughing, she thought.

"It's probably just Mia," she said, sounding calm and cool. "Remember, she was going to try to find some music to play."

"That doesn't sound like Mia's music," Jason said doubtfully.

Tracy never knew Jason was such a good actor. He almost had her convinced. "Mia's music is pretty weird," she said. "Now, I'm going back down to write these notes again, so why don't you go brush your teeth?"

Her head high, she started down the stairs. Hah, she thought. I might not be a genius, but I'm not a total idiot, either.

Left behind on the third-floor landing, Jason stared after Tracy. She should have been scared, he thought, swallowing the dry lump in his throat. I'm scared, so why isn't she?

Back down on the second floor, Tracy couldn't wait to get to her room and tell Nora and Jennifer about the boys' latest "ghost." She was hurrying along the hall, when she suddenly realized that the weird music was still going on. Not only that, it was louder.

For one awful second, Tracy froze, her heart pounding and her hands crumpling the already-wrinkled notes. The only thing to do, she thought, was scream. But just as she opened her mouth to do it, she remembered the explanation she'd given to Jason — it was Mia, playing her awful punk music, trying to find something that wouldn't make the two teachers grit their teeth and tear their hair and get madder at each other than they already were.

It wasn't a trick after all, she thought, as her legs unfroze and she started down the hall again. But it wasn't a ghost, either. Still, being terrified twice in ten minutes was just too much. Let everybody else rave about how great Mandeville Manor was. She, for one, would be perfectly happy if she never saw it again.

* * *

Inside the room she shared with Susan, Denise, and Lucy, Mia pulled a pair of purple leather boots out of her suitcase. They were cut low, just above the ankle, with fringes on the back and silver insets in the shape of snakes running up the sides. They were new and she was going to wear them to the play tomorrow. But the rain had started again — she could hear it pattering against the window — and there was no way she'd wear these boots without waterproofing them first.

"What are you doing, Mia?" Denise asked, as Mia took a can from her suitcase and started shaking it.

"Waterproofing," Mia said. "Can't you hear the rain? I don't want these to get ruined."

"I know, but I thought you were going to try to find some music," Denise said, brushing out her long blonde hair.

"Something not too outrageous," Lucy added.

"Which is probably impossible," Susan said. "But don't you think you ought to try anyway? For all we know, Mr. Rochester and Ms. Spencer might already be having their rendezvous in the dining room."

"Well, they'll have to have it without music," Mia said, "because my tape recorder's broken."

Chapter 12

By the time Tracy sat down to write her second set of notes, the rain was coming down harder. As Jeff had told Jennifer, there was thunder and lightning with it, too, as well as a strong wind that moaned and shrieked and whipped the leaves off the trees outside.

"I wish they hadn't put the fire out," Jennifer said, glancing at the fireplace. "A fire would feel really cozy right now with all that weather going on."

"It would be nice," Nora agreed, reading the two notes. Tracy's spelling tended to be shaky, and since they were supposed to be from teachers, Nora thought they should be proofread. "But I guess they can't take any chances." The notes were fine, so she put them into envelopes.

"Well, I'm not taking any chances this time, either," Tracy said. She stood up from the dressing table and smoothed out her pink angora sweater. "I'm not going up to that third floor alone again and maybe be scared again and wreck these notes again."

"But I thought you said the music was Mia's," Nora told her.

"I did," Tracy said. "But I've decided that boys can't be trusted, not when they're in groups, anyway. And if they're lying in wait up there to play another trick, I want company. Besides," she went on indignantly, "I've been doing all the work so far."

"She's right," Jennifer said to Nora.

"Sorry, Tracy," Nora said. "Just let us change and we'll go upstairs with you."

"Great," Tracy said, relieved. "But why do you have to change?"

"Are you kidding?" Nora said, going over to the armoire. "There's no way I'm going to let any of those guys see me in a pair of Dr. Denton's!"

A few minutes later, back in their pants and sweaters, Jennifer and Nora tiptoed up the stairs with Tracy.

"I feel like a fat yellow chicken," Nora whispered to Jennifer. She hadn't been able to face putting on her oil-stained sweater again, so she'd borrowed one from Tracy — a bright yellow bulky one that wasn't right for her height. "A short, fat, yellow chicken."

Jennifer giggled. "Actually, you look more like a neon light," she whispered back. "If we have a power failure, we'll use you to see by."

"Don't mention power failure," Tracy hissed over her shoulder. "This creepy house is dark enough."

When they got to the third floor, the hall was as quiet and dim as when Tracy had been up there half an hour before. Pressing her finger to her lips, she motioned for the other two to follow her, and on tiptoe, they all crept down the hall to Mr. Rochester's door.

Carefully, so the paper wouldn't crackle, Tracy lifted her right hand and held the note out to Nora.

Nora pointed to herself and raised her eyebrows in a questioning look.

Tracy nodded and held out her hand. It was shaking slightly. "Doctors are supposed to have steady hands," she breathed softly, her lips barely moving. "You do it."

Taking the note and a deep breath, Nora bent down and carefully slid the envelope through the crack under the door. Then the three of them raced silently in stockinged feet for the stairs.

"Phase One, half complete," Jennifer said on

the way down to the second floor.

"Thank goodness," Tracy sighed.

"I just thought of something," Nora said, stopping on the steps. "What if he's asleep?"

Jennifer checked her watch. It was a quarter to ten. "He said he had papers to grade," she reminded them. "Anyway, if he is asleep, there's nothing we can do about it. Come on, let's deliver the next note and wait to see what happens."

Being careful to keep her hand steady, Nora slid Ms. Spencer's note under her bedroom door. Just as she was straightening up, she heard something.

It was music — very odd music, like a very old record being played inside a very large tin can.

Nora and Jennifer both looked at Tracy. "Is that what you heard?" Nora asked her.

Tracy listened for a few seconds and finally shrugged. "It's hard to tell," she said. "All I remember is that it was very strange."

"You're right about that," Jennifer agreed. "This music is weird! We'd better tell Mia that she's way off track."

When the girls went into the others' room, they found Lucy still dressed, lying on the bed, reading a fashion magazine. Susan was in the shower; Denise was putting on a sort of jumpsuit in shocking pink that looked more like a lounging outfit than pajamas. And Mia was sitting in one of the armchairs, fiddling with her tape recorder.

"Well?" Denise asked expectantly. "Is the deed done?"

Jennifer nodded. "The notes are delivered. Now we wait for the fun to start."

Lucy laughed. "I don't know whether it'll be fun or not, but it sure will be interesting."

Jennifer looked at Mia and started to say something, but Mia interrupted her. "I just don't get it," she muttered, tapping the recorder with her long magenta nail. "I've tried absolutely everything and nothing works."

"That's okay," Jennifer told her, thinking that Mia was talking about the music. "Forget it. It was a good idea, but we don't have to have it."

"Especially whatever it was you were just playing," Tracy said. "What group was that, anyway? They sounded like they were playing tin cans."

Mia looked up, confused. "What are you talking about?"

"The music we heard just a minute ago." Nora shook her head and laughed. "You said it didn't work and boy, Mia, were you right!"

Mia, Denise, and Lucy looked at each other

and raised their eyebrows. Jennifer caught the look and said, "Wait a minute. I get the feeling we're talking about two different things. We were talking about the music. What were you talking about?"

Mia held up the recorder. "I was talking about this. It's on the blink."

"Oh, so that's why the music sounded so weird," Tracy said.

"What music?" Mia asked, sounding exasperated. "I just said, my recorder's broken. It won't play."

"Which is not exactly a tragedy," Susan said, coming in from the bathroom with a fluffy white towel around her head.

This time, it was Nora, Jennifer, and Tracy who raised their eyebrows at each other.

"I see we're still not communicating," Lucy remarked, tossing her magazine aside.

"I guess not. Um . . . Mia," Jennifer said slowly, "are you telling us you haven't been playing any music at all?"

"Not since before dinner," Mia said.

"But we heard music out in the hall just a minute ago!" Tracy protested. "It had to be yours! Who else — ?" She stopped and gave a little gasp.

For a moment, they all stared at each other, not sure what to think. Then Nora gave herself a little shake. "If you guys are thinking what I was just thinking . . ."

"The ghost!" Tracy whispered.

". . . then we're all being ridiculous," Nora finished. "Calm down, Tracy. There is no ghost. But there are a bunch of guys upstairs who want us to believe there's a ghost."

"Of course," Denise said, pulling her hair back and fastening it with a wide silver clip. "They've tried two times to scare us and they haven't been able to. We should have known they'd try again."

"Let's just ignore them this time," Lucy suggested, fluffing up her pillow and yawning. "Pretty soon they'll get bored and then we can all get some sleep."

Everyone — even Tracy — agreed, and just as she, Jennifer, and Nora were starting to leave, there was a knock on the door.

"It's them," Nora said positively. "They haven't heard us screaming in terror yet, and they can't stand it, so they came to find out why." She walked toward the door. "Be cool," she whispered, and pulled the door open.

Standing in the hallway was Steve Crowley, barefoot, wearing a T-shirt and jeans.

Susan dodged back behind the bathroom door, not wanting him to see her in a bathrobe with her hair all wet and tangled, but Steve didn't even notice.

"Good, everybody's still awake," he said.

"Not for long," Lucy called out.

"What is it Steve?" Nora asked innocently.

He ran his fingers through his hair a little nervously. "I know you're not going to believe this, but — "

"You're right," Mia interrupted. "We're not going to believe it."

"We were afraid of that," Steve said. "So we decided to ask if you'd come up and see for yourselves."

"See?" Denise asked coolly. "Don't you mean 'hear'?"

Steve nodded in surprise. "How did you know?"

Nora laughed. "When are you guys going to give up?" she asked. "We heard the music, Steve. It was a nice try, but it didn't work. The game's over, so good-night." She started to push the door shut.

"Wait! I wasn't talking about music!" Steve called out, blocking the door with his hand. "We didn't hear music. Well, Jason said he did, but nobody believed him. No, what we heard was laughter!"

Jennifer was quiet, watching him. At first,

she'd thought he was joking, but now she wasn't so sure. Steve liked to joke as much as anybody, but she had a strange feeling that this time, he was serious.

She walked over and took his hand. "Come on," she said to the others. "Let's go see what this is all about."

Five minutes later, the eighth-graders were gathered in the third-floor hallway. All the girls except Jennifer were still skeptical, but they couldn't help wanting to know how the boys had managed this trick. The boys, however, didn't seem to be hamming it up as much as before. In fact, they were extremely quiet.

Susan, having hastily run a comb through her wet hair and put her clothes back on, was counting heads. All the boys were in the hallway. "Maybe one of them learned how to throw his voice," she whispered to Denise.

Denise nodded. She'd pulled an oversized sweater on over her pajamas and except for her stockinged feet, she looked good enough to go on a date. "When the laughter starts, keep your eyes on their lips," she said.

"*If* the laughter starts," Lucy corrected.

"I wish it would start," Susan complained loudly. "I'm getting awfully sleepy!"

"Ssh!" Tommy hissed. "If it happens again

it'll be real quiet at first, so don't make too much noise or you might miss it."

Nora felt a slight shiver run down her spine. Tommy just wasn't behaving normally. He was quiet and tense and he hadn't combed his hair a single time. In fact, none of the guys were acting the way she'd expected. They didn't seem to care whether anyone believed them or not. She glanced at Jen, who was standing next to Steve and looking worried. She feels it, too, Nora thought.

"I hate to admit this," she whispered, "but I've suddenly got the creeps."

"Ssh," Tommy said again. "I think I hear it. Listen."

At first, all anyone could hear was the wind and rain outside. But then, one by one, everyone heard a third sound — a ripple of laughter, like a child's giggle. It lasted for just a few seconds, then stopped. Nobody breathed.

When the laughter started again, it wasn't soft and giggly anymore. It was still high-pitched, though, and as they listened, it quickly grew louder until it turned into a wild, hysterical shriek.

Chapter 13

The second round of laughter died as suddenly as it had started, leaving a stunned silence in its wake. No one moved or spoke for a full minute. Tracy would have felt much better if she could have screamed, but her voice seemed to have deserted her, so she had to be satisfied with keeping her eyes squeezed shut and her hands over her ears.

Susan tried to think of something insulting to say, but for once, her sharp tongue failed her. Besides, there was nobody to insult.

It was Jason who finally broke the silence. Standing there in a striped pajama top tucked into his jeans, clutching his skateboard to his skinny chest, he looked warily up and down the hall, then said, "Was that animal, vegetable, or human?"

Nobody laughed, but they all stopped standing like statues and started breathing again. Nora straightened her shoulders and turned to Steve.

"You guys get Mr. Rochester," she said, surprised that her voice actually sounded normal. "We'll get Ms. Spencer. Meet us down on the second floor."

Everyone moved, relieved to have something to do.

"Are you mildly scared or totally terrified?" Jennifer asked Nora as the girls headed downstairs.

"Somewhere in between," Nora said, jumping the last three steps and landing smoothly.

"Me, too!" Jennifer jumped after her.

"Well, I'm totally terrified!" Tracy had finally found her voice. "How fast do you think we can get out of here?"

"Who said anything about leaving?" Nora called back over her shoulder as she raced for Ms. Spencer's room. "I'm not leaving until I find out who was laughing!"

"Oh, no!" Tracy wailed. "I knew you were going to say that!"

"If it makes you feel any better, Tracy," Mia confessed, "I'm not too thrilled about sticking around, either!"

Reaching Ms. Spencer's door, Nora raised her fist and hammered on it. Everyone waited breathlessly, but no one came to the door.

"Knock louder!" Tracy urged. "She must be asleep."

Again, Nora pounded on the door, long and hard. "There," she said, rubbing her knuckles, "that was loud enough to wake the — "

"Don't say that word!" Tracy pleaded.

Nora couldn't help laughing. "I was going to say 'the soundest sleeper.' Tracy, calm down, you're getting hysterical."

"Let her," Susan suggested. "We need some comic relief."

"Well, Susan," Lucy commented dryly, "I can see you're back to normal."

"Is it my imagination," Denise asked, "or is Ms. Spencer's door still closed?"

Jennifer pounded on it this time. Still no answer. "Should I open it?"

"Go ahead," Nora said. "We have to tell her about this. I just hope she isn't in the middle of a fantastic dream when we wake her up."

Ms. Spencer wasn't dreaming, though. In fact, she wasn't in the room at all, and the light was off in the adjoining bathroom. The note Tracy had written was still lying just inside the door.

"She never got it," Tracy whispered mournfully.

Before anyone could try to convince Tracy that Ms. Spencer hadn't been spirited away, they heard the sound of pounding feet as the boys came rushing down the stairs.

"Mr. Rochester's not there," Steve reported. "Where's Ms. Spencer?"

"Vanished," Jennifer said. "Sorry, Tracy," she added quickly, "I didn't mean it that way."

"What about the note?" Nora asked.

"What note?" Jason said, still clutching his skateboard.

"The apology note," Nora reminded him. "Was it still on the floor?"

"We weren't looking at the floor," Mitch told her.

"Well, never mind," Nora said. "They've got to be somewhere in the house, so let's find them."

Jennifer smiled as they all headed for the stairs leading to the main floor. Nora's so good at calming everybody down, she thought proudly. And she might get scared, but she never stopped thinking. So if there were any ghosts, they'd better look out. Nora Ryan could out-think them all.

The large entrance hall was dark except for one small dim lamp. Every few seconds a flash of lightning would brighten it up, but the thunder that followed made everyone jumpy.

"I wish this storm would hurry up and stop," Tracy complained.

"But Tracy," Steve teased, "what's a haunted house without a thunderstorm to make it even scarier?"

"See?" Tracy said to everyone. "Steve thinks it's haunted, too!"

"He was joking, Tracy," Denise explained. "And this house is not haunted. It's just . . . noisy."

"I read something somewhere about noisy ghosts," Andy commented. "I can't remember the name, though."

Lucy nodded. "Poltergeist."

"*Gesundheit*," Jason said.

"No, Jason, I didn't sneeze. I said — " Lucy stopped. "Wait. Do you hear that?"

Everyone listened. Over the sounds of the wind and thunder came another sound — knocking.

"The dining room," Nora said. "Come on."

The knocking was coming from inside the dining room. And from behind its big door, which was now shut, they heard the voices of Mr. Rochester and Ms. Spencer.

"Anybody out there?" Mr. Rochester called.

"Yes!" Nora shouted back. "We're *all* out here!"

"The door's locked," Ms. Spencer called. "Get Miss Mandeville, will you please?"

"It's not locked, it's just stuck," the students heard Mr. Rochester say to her. To them he said, "Get something to pry it open with."

Jennifer and Nora looked at each other. Operation Lovesave obviously wasn't working yet.

The door did turn out to be locked, but there was no need to get Miss Mandeville. The key was still in it, on the hall side. With one smooth turn, Nora had the door open.

As the students poured into the dining room, everyone started talking at once, telling about the strange music and the wild laughter. Once they finally got the story straight, the teachers looked as mystified as everyone else.

"I wish I'd heard it," Mr. Rochester said.

"No you don't," Mia said. "It was awful. Be glad you were stuck down here."

"Well, that's another thing," Tracy pointed out. "Just how exactly did that dining room door get locked — from the outside?"

"Maybe the key was turned anyway, so when they shut it, it locked automatically," Nora suggested.

The two teachers exchanged glances and finally Ms. Spencer cleared her throat. "Here's what happened," she said. "I got hungry and came down to see if there was still some fruit in here."

"And I couldn't concentrate," Mr. Rochester told them, "so I brought my papers downstairs." He pointed to a stack of essays on one of the tables.

"When was this, anyway?" Jennifer asked.

"Oh, about nine-fifteen, I think," Mr. Rochester said.

"And I came down about half an hour later," Ms. Spencer said. "Why?"

"Just like to keep things in order," Jen said quickly.

Nora hid a smile. Jen didn't care about order — she wanted to know about the notes. But nine-fifteen was when Tracy was rewriting them, and nine forty-five was when they'd delivered Mr. Rochester's. So both notes were still lying on the floor upstairs.

"It's eleven now," Tracy said, looking appalled. "You mean you two have been locked in here all that time?"

Mr. Rochester nodded. "Almost."

Jennifer cheered up a little. They might not have fallen into each other's arms yet, but at least they hadn't broken each other's heads. There was still a chance, she thought hopefully.

"Anyway," Ms. Spencer went on, "we'd been

in here a few minutes, when suddenly the door just . . . slammed shut."

"By itself?" Mia asked.

"It seemed that way," Mr. Rochester admitted.

The students couldn't help looking at Mitch, who'd had the idea of locking the two of them in a room together in the first place. But Mitch hadn't done it, they knew that. He was as scared and confused as the rest of them. If he could have explained how the door got shut and locked, he would have.

"I have an idea," Steve said. "This is an old house. Maybe the whole thing's a little tilted or something and every once in a while, the door just shuts. That can happen. Of course," he admitted, "it doesn't explain the laughter."

"Or the music," Tracy added. "Anyway, I don't see why everybody wants to find out what happened."

"Aren't you the least bit curious?" Susan asked.

"Maybe, but I'm a bigger bit scared," Tracy said. "What I'd really like to do is leave."

Mr. Rochester smiled. "I don't blame you for feeling that way, Tracy," he said, walking over to the table where he'd put his papers. "I'd be a little scared myself if I'd heard what the rest of you did."

As he was talking, Mr. Rochester reached for the papers, and just as he did, the table slid six inches across the floor. He stopped, his hand still outstretched. Then he blinked and took a step toward the table, which just as suddenly shot back toward him.

" 'They're back.' " Tommy tried to joke, quoting from the movie *Poltergeist II*.

No one laughed, not even Tommy. Like everyone else, his eyes were glued to the table, which was now moving back and forth as if it had a life of its own.

Nora was frowning. "There's something really strange about the way that table's moving," she muttered.

"There's something really strange about a table moving in the first place!" Mia said.

"I know, but I meant. . . ," Nora shook her head. "I'm not sure." Before she could decide what it was that bothered her, the table came to a sudden stop, back in its original position.

"Well," Ms. Spencer said after a few seconds, "this is turning out to be quite a night, isn't it?"

"And it's not over yet," Jason whispered. "Look."

Everyone looked to where he was pointing, which was at a painting on one of the walls. Because of the mechanic's story, they weren't totally surprised to see the painting tilt one way and then the other, as if an unseen hand were trying to get it straight.

Like the table, the painting kept moving for about half a minute, then stopped.

Everyone turned to the sideboard. After all, the music, the laughter, the painting stories had come true. If everything went like it was supposed to, then the sideboard would be next.

But the sideboard stayed right where it was. And just when everyone's heartbeat was starting to return to normal, there was a deafening crack of thunder, followed almost immediately by a bolt of lightning; the lights flickered, then went out completely, and the dining room was in total darkness.

Chapter 14

After everything else that had gone on that night, the lights going out didn't even cause a single eyebrow to raise. In fact, in the lightning flashes that followed, Jennifer could see that a lot of them were actually smiling.

"I guess it had to happen," she said with a grin. "It was just a matter of time."

"And the timing was perfect — right out of a horror movie!" Steve quipped.

"No, it wasn't," Denise laughed. "This was a natural phenomenon, remember?"

"Finally!" Mia said. "I've had enough of the other kind!"

Not only was everyone smiling now, most of them were laughing. Even Tracy, who had thought she'd pass out if the power failed, couldn't resist joining in.

"I'm not sure why we're laughing," she said. "But I guess it's better than screaming."

"Laughter is a perfectly natural reaction." Nora tried to sound doctorly and wound up giggling. "I mean, what else can you do when things get so ridiculous?"

"We could try finding some candles," Mr. Rochester chuckled. "If that table starts moving again, I'd like to make sure my shins are out of its path."

"I agree," Tommy said. "We need to shed more light on the subject."

Everyone groaned and then, still laughing, they started searching around the room, bumping into the furniture and each other, trying to find candles.

"There's one," Jason called out. "It's already lit, too, isn't that convenient?"

"What do you mean, it's already — " Susan stopped in mid-sentence. Through the open dining room doors, out in the hall, she saw a candle flickering and growing brighter as the shadowy figure carrying it came closer and closer.

"I see it, too," Mia whispered.

"And we thought it was all over," Lucy said. "Who do you think it is?"

"Lady Macbeth, who else?" said Mitch, who

was closest to the doors and recognized the candle-carrier. "Quiet, guys, she's sleepwalking, you know."

"Hello?" Judith Mandeville called out, stopping in the doorway and holding the wavering candle high so she could see better.

"Very funny, Mitch," Lucy said. "You could have told us who it was."

"Yeah, but it was more fun not to," he said.

Miss Mandeville came slowly into the room, one hand cupped in front of the candle flame to keep it from going out. "I never did understand how people do this," she said, moving in a very slow shuffle and keeping her eyes on the candle. "I always wind up getting hot wax on my hand." She stopped and lifted the candle again, looking around.

"Goodness!" she exclaimed. "You're all here!"

"We were just . . . uh . . ." Jason started.

". . . having a meeting," Nora finished.

"Well, that makes it easy," Miss Mandeville said. "When the lights went out, I thought I'd better bring everyone some flashlights and candles. You'll find candles and holders in the sideboard drawers." She patted the now-bulging pockets of her gray cardigan, which she was wearing over a long flannel nightgown. "And I've got six mini-flashlights in here."

In just a few minutes, there was a candle on every surface, and the room took on a rosy, mellow glow.

"This is so romantic," Tracy sighed. "It almost makes me forget everything else that's happened."

"Oh, I know what you mean," Miss Mandeville commiserated. "A power failure's a terrible nuisance."

Everyone exchanged glances, and Mr. Rochester cleared his throat. "To be honest, Miss Mandeville," he said, "I'm afraid the power failure is just one of several nuisances."

" 'Nuisance' is putting it mildly," Susan muttered under her breath.

"Oh, dear." Miss Mandeville looked very concerned. "If there's something about the service that isn't satisfactory, I do wish you'd tell me. I'll be more than happy to take care of it."

"The service has been wonderful," Ms. Spencer assured her. "Please don't worry about that."

"Then I'm afraid I don't understand."

"I think the students should tell you," Ms. Spencer said. "They saw and heard more than Mr. Rochester and I did."

Miss Mandeville turned toward the eighth-graders, her expression curious and expectant.

"Let's let Nora tell her," Jennifer suggested.

"Thanks a lot," Nora said.

"Come on, you're always good at getting the details right and keeping things straight." And Nora wouldn't exaggerate or be superdramatic either, Jennifer thought, something which would probably keep Miss Mandeville from believing them. Not that the story needed any exaggeration. It was already weird enough.

Nora paused, organizing her thoughts. "Well," she said, "it all started about nine o'clock. And it started with music."

A few minutes later, the story was told. Nora had kept everything straight and in order, and the others had helped her out with descriptions from time to time. Nobody exaggerated or got melodramatic; the story came out sounding like an oral book report, except for one thing — this wasn't fiction.

When they'd finished, Miss Mandeville sat quietly for a moment, staring straight ahead, but not really looking at anything. Then she sighed deeply.

"Well, I'm afraid that's that," she said quietly. "I'm just going to have to close Mandeville Manor down."

No one was expecting to hear that.

"It isn't going to be easy," she went on, almost as if she were talking to herself. "This house means a lot to me. But it has to be done."

Jennifer felt terrible. "But Miss Mandeville," she said sympathetically, "we didn't mean for you to do that. I mean, that's not why we told you what happened."

"Oh, yes, I know," Miss Mandeville told her. "But you see, you're the first guests I've had in a long, long time. And after tonight, I'm not likely to get anymore."

"Then we won't tell anyone," Jennifer said impulsively.

"Right," Tommy agreed. "Our lips are sealed."

Miss Mandeville laughed, and some of the sparkle came back into her eyes. "That's a wonderful suggestion," she said. "I wish all my other guests had kept their lips sealed. But," she went on, "I think it's too late now. I don't mind admitting that Mandeville Manor is losing money at an alarming rate."

"Didn't you say you had a brother?" Denise asked. "Maybe he could help."

"That wouldn't be very likely." Miss Mandeville paused, looking a little embarrassed. Then she went on, "You see, my parents left this house only to me. My father wanted James to follow in his footsteps and become a banker, but James had a mind of his own. He was always very clever, always trying to invent new gadgets. I believe he had some success, but not enough to satisfy Father. At any rate, when my parents died, and it was discovered that I was the sole inheritor, James went off to Europe in quite a huff." She smiled. "I don't think he'd be in much of a hurry to help me out."

"I almost wish we hadn't told you what happened," Mia said.

"Oh, no, I'm glad you did," Miss Mandeville said. "The other guests did, too, of course, but they weren't nearly as considerate about it as you've been."

"Did you ever try to find out what was wrong?" Nora asked.

Miss Mandeville nodded. "Every time," she said. "The strangest thing is that it never happens while I'm here alone. Only when I have guests. I don't suppose I'll ever know now." She sighed again, and then stood up. "Well," she said, more briskly, "you're welcome to stay down here for the rest of the night if it would make you more at ease. I'm going back to my rooms, but I'll leave these here." She pulled the flashlights from her pockets, set them on a table, then picked up a candle and walked toward the door.

"I do hope nothing else happens," she said, turning back for a moment. "But if it does, please call me. I wouldn't mind seeing some of it for myself!"

"That's so sad," Tracy said when she'd gone.

"I know," Jennifer agreed. "It's not fair."

"I've got an idea," Mitch said. "When we leave, we spread the word about what a fantastic place this is."

"Especially how calm and quiet and peaceful it is," Lucy added with a grin.

"How bored we got because nothing happened," Tommy said. "No, wait, that wouldn't help."

Ms. Spencer smiled. "I admire your instincts," she said to them all, "but I'm not sure that will solve the problem."

Mr. Rochester nodded. "Mandeville Manor needs more than one group of satisfied guests, I'm afraid."

"Hey, your family's rich, Denise," Jason said to her. "Maybe they could spread the word to some of their rich friends to come and stay here."

"Are you kidding?" Susan asked scornfully. "They go to places like the Riviera, not to a podunk town like Piedmont."

"Well, it was just an idea," Jason muttered. Boy, he thought, Susan sure knew how to make a guy feel like a worm. And the thing was, he really did want to help Miss Mandeville. He liked her. He liked that sweater of hers, too, with those deep pockets. Pockets like that would come in very handy. Too bad nobody but grown-ups wore those sweaters. He could use one, but he wouldn't dare. Susan would hang him out to dry.

When Jason's thoughts finally twisted their way to an end, he looked up to see Denise smiling at him.

"It really wasn't such a ridiculous idea, Jason," she said, thinking that for all his faults, Jason at least had a decent heart. "But the same thing might happen to my family and their friends that happened to us. Then Miss Mandeville would be right back where she started."

Jason blinked, not because he didn't understand what she was saying, but because the beautiful Denise Hendrix was actually smiling at him. At him, Jason Anthony. He wasn't sure why she was smiling, but he didn't want to press his luck by asking. So he gave her a lop-sided grin and kept his mouth shut.

"There must be something we can do to help!" Jennifer said. "I just hate the thought of leaving here, knowing she's going to have to close it down."

"I think Jennifer just found another cause," Lucy said with a grin.

"I did," Jennifer admitted. "But if I can't think of anything to do, then it's a lost cause."

"It's not lost yet, Jen," Nora said quickly. "It's only midnight, you know. That gives us at least seven or eight hours."

"Of sleep?" Tracy asked.

"No, of time," Nora said. "Look, we all know there's no ghost." She looked sternly at Tracy. "Don't we?"

"Oh, I guess," Tracy admitted. "But there's something strange, that's for sure."

Jason, who was sitting cross-legged on the floor, reached out and pulled his skateboard into his lap. Tapping it softly like a drum, he started chanting the words to *Ghostbusters*.

Tommy said, "Hey, right! We'll be — "

"Ghostbusters!" Nora cried.

"Oh, come on," Susan said to Nora. "You really think we can find out what's been going on?"

"I think we can try," Nora told her.

"So do I," Jennifer said loyally. When she and Nora got behind the same cause, they made a great team. And if everybody helped, they just might be unbeatable.

Susan was about to make a sarcastic remark about Jennifer and Nora always sticking up for each other. But she stopped herself. The Bobbsey Twins were doing something she was interested in, for once. She really did want to know what was going on in this house.

"Well," she said, "I guess it won't hurt to poke around a little bit."

"She's really dying of curiosity," Mia whispered to Denise. "She just won't admit it since she didn't come up with the idea first."

"Poke around?" Tracy asked a little fearfully. "Is that what you're going to do?"

Nora grinned. "No, Tracy, that's what *we're* going to do. All of us."

"Together," Jennifer added quickly, before Tracy got too nervous. "Or in groups, anyway."

"Let's have a planning session," Nora said. She looked at the teachers. "This is all right with you, isn't it?"

"I think it's a great idea," Ms. Spencer said. "In fact, I think I'll join in."

"I wouldn't miss it, either," Mr. Rochester said.

"Great!" Nora said. "Then let's figure out what we're going to do."

"And remember," Mitch said, holding a flashlight under his chin and grinning evilly, "if anybody sees a ghost, 'who ya gonna call?'"

"'Ghostbusters!'" they all shouted.

Chapter 15

It was almost one in the morning before everyone finished planning their strategy and set out on their mission to lay the Ghost of Mandeville Manor to rest for good.

No one knew exactly what they were looking for, but they were determined to find something. Music and laughter didn't just happen; there had to be a reason. Maybe it wasn't really music and laughter, but powerful radio signals that got trapped and distorted in Mandeville Manor's lightning rods or antennas at certain times of the night.

The sliding picture and table were something else, of course. The house might be tilted, but it wouldn't keep on tilting like a seesaw. Unless, as Jason suggested, there was a giant troll underneath the house, getting his exercise.

"Just check out everything," Nora said, as

they divided into groups and filed out of the dining room. "The walls, the lamps and the light fixtures, the furniture, everything. We'll find something, I just know it."

The question is, What? Tracy wondered as she followed her group up to the third floor. Normally, she would have been totally thrilled. Besides her, the third floor group consisted of Mitch, Andy, and Mr. Rochester. One man, two boys, and Tracy Douglas. Andy didn't count, since he was Mia's boyfriend and a little too odd, anyway. And Mr. Rochester was engaged, or he had been the last time she'd looked at Ms. Spencer's ring finger. But Mitch Pauley! He was so cute!

It should have been heaven, being in a group with three guys, even if two of them were unavailable. It was exactly the kind of situation Tracy dreamed about. Except the dream had never taken place in a dark house where all kinds of creepy things might happen any minute.

I won't be scared, Tracy said to herself as they reached the third floor. Then she thought, Maybe I will! If I'm scared, maybe Mitch will get protective. That's what boys were supposed to do. She smiled to herself. This might not be so bad after all.

They weren't using candles, not wanting to

burn the house down before they found out what was going on in it, so each group had two flashlights. Mr. Rochester had one of them, and Tracy, bringing up the rear, was carrying the other. When they got to the third floor hall, Mr. Rochester and Andy went in to search one of the bedrooms, leaving Tracy and Mitch together in the hall. Perfect, Tracy thought.

"Mitch," she said, letting her voice tremble a little, "what if that horrible laughing starts again?"

"Gosh, that would be great," he said, taking the light from her and aiming it at the ceiling.

"It would?"

"Uh-huh. When it happened before, I was too scared to do anything but listen to it," Mitch explained. "If it starts again, though, we might be able to figure out where it's coming from." He turned, aiming the flashlight right at her face. "Tracy, didn't it seem like the laughter just sort of filled the whole hall?"

Tracy tried to keep up her helpless, frightened act, even though she knew she didn't look good squinting. "Yes, it just surrounded us," she agreed breathlessly. "It was one of the worst moments of my life. That's why I just hope it doesn't happen again."

"Mmm." Mitch finally moved the beam of the flashlight from her face and shone it on the three light fixtures spaced evenly along the hall ceiling. "Hey, Trace, could you get me a chair?"

"You want me to get you a chair?" Tracy said slowly. This wasn't going the way it was supposed to.

"Yeah, I just had an idea about those lights."

"And you want me to get you a chair?" Tracy repeated.

"Right, so I can get up there and take a look," Mitch said. He walked down the hall, shining his light on each of the overhead fixtures. When he turned back, Tracy was still standing where he'd left her. "Tracy?" he said, aiming the light at her face again. "What about the chair?"

Boys, Tracy thought disgustedly. They didn't recognize a romantic moment even when it was handed to them on a platter. "Oh, all right," she pouted. "I'll get your stupid chair!"

What did I do? Mitch wondered, as Tracy stomped off. All he'd done was ask for a chair. She was awfully touchy. She must really be scared. Well, she wasn't the only one.

On the second floor, which was the territory assigned to Ms. Spencer, Denise, Lucy, and Tommy, there was no confusion at all about what anyone was thinking. The girls and Ms. Spencer were completely businesslike. Tommy had tried to liven things up a little by cracking

156

ghost jokes, but all he'd gotten for his trouble were three cool looks. He took the hint and from then on, kept himself busy taking lamps apart, looking behind paintings, and checking for any wires that didn't seem to lead anywhere.

"I just remembered something," Lucy said, when they'd all gathered out in the hall. "Nora and Jen and Tracy were right out here when they heard the music. If it had been coming from one of the rooms, they would have noticed that, wouldn't they?"

Ms. Spencer shone her flashlight around the hall and up to the ceiling. "Let's take a look at those light fixtures," she said. "They're the only things where any kind of sound could come from."

Denise turned to Tommy. "Bring us a chair, would you please?"

"At your service, madam," Tommy said. "Anything else? Some tea? Perhaps some crumpets?"

"Just the chair," Denise said dryly.

"Very good, madam." Tommy bowed from the waist and went off to get the chair. Obviously, they didn't appreciate his sense of humor. Oh well, at least he was getting some exercise.

* * *

While the upstairs groups were closing in on the hall ceilings, the downstairs group had divided into two groups. Jennifer, Mia, and Steve were searching the kitchen and two other rooms, while Nora, Jason, and Susan concentrated on the dining room.

In the flickering candlelight, Nora and Jason grabbed hold of the table that had moved and turned it over.

"What are those?" Jason asked, pointing to three metal pieces attached to the bottom of the table legs.

"Casters," Nora said. "They make it easier to move."

"They sure did work tonight," Jason commented.

"I've heard of casters on furniture," Susan said from across the room. "But did you ever see them on paintings?"

She'd taken the painting off the wall; on the back, at the bottom, was a piece of metal just like the ones on the table legs.

Jason frowned at it. "Maybe it's a new way of hanging pictures. Zap it to the wall with a magnet."

"Magnets!" Nora cried. "That's it! That's what I thought of when the table was moving — it looked like something was holding it to the floor."

"But these aren't magnets," Susan said, holding the metal flashlight against the bottom of the painting. "See? It doesn't stick."

"I know, but there could be a magnet behind the wall," Nora said. "Or underneath. . . ." She stopped and looked down at the floor. Slowly, she said, "Does Mandeville Manor have a basement?"

No one knew, but before they could go to see, the upstairs search parties rushed into the dining room.

"Evidence!" Mitch cried, holding something up in his hand. "This ghost not only makes noise, it uses stereo equipment to do it!"

"It's a microcassette," Andy said, as everyone gathered around Mitch. "I can't tell what brand, but it's the latest. Its speaker is probably almost as good as the ones I've got in my room at home."

"Mitch and Tracy found it in the hall ceiling," Denise said. "And we found one on the second floor. The only thing is, we can't get them to play."

"The controls are on them," Andy said. "But there must be some central, remote button that — "

"Remote?" Nora interrupted. "Did you say remote?"

Andy nodded. "People do it all the time," he

said. "Set up systems all over their houses with a central control."

"What is it, Nora?" Mr. Rochester asked. "I can tell you've got a theory."

Nora quickly explained what they'd found on the table legs and behind the painting. "If Mandeville Manor has a basement," she finished, "I think we ought to take a look at what's down there."

"It has a basement, all right," Steve said, coming into the room with Mia and Jennifer. "And it's dark. Very dark."

"None of us wanted to go down," Jennifer said. "The steps are steep and it's dark as a dungeon. That's why we came to get you. What's going on, anyway?"

"Plenty," Lucy said, and told them what they'd discovered.

When she'd finished, Jennifer said, "I guess there's only one thing to do."

"Don't tell me, let me guess," Tracy said miserably. "We're going down to the dungeon."

"Cheer up, Tracy," Lucy laughed. "This night can't last forever."

"Should we tell Miss Mandeville?" Mia asked.

"Let's wait," Mr. Rochester suggested. "She's probably asleep, so let's leave her alone until we see if there's anything downstairs."

"There has to be," Nora said excitedly. "I can just feel it!"

"I thought doctors weren't supposed to rely on intuition," Susan remarked.

"I'm not a doctor yet," Nora grinned. "I can still rely on anything I like."

Single file, with the flashlights spread out among them, they left the dining room and went across the entrance hall into the kitchen.

"That's the door to the basement," Mia said quietly, pointing across the room. "But don't ask me to go first."

Nora clutched her flashlight tightly. "I'll go first," she volunteered. She wasn't crazy about dark, dungeonlike places, but at the moment she was more curious than scared. Besides, she reminded herself, in spite of all the strange things that had happened, no one had been hurt. Whatever the ghost was, it wasn't violent.

Taking a deep breath, Nora reached out and pulled open the basement door. The second she did, she felt something brush against her leg. She didn't scream, but she gasped so loud it might as well have been a scream. But she couldn't help it — whatever had touched her was alive!

Chapter 16

"What is it, what is it?!" Tracy cried from somewhere near the back of the line.

"Good question!" Nora said, finally able to speak. "It moved, that's all I know."

"It's still moving," Jennifer laughed, "but don't worry, it's not a monster."

All six flashlights were suddenly aimed at Jennifer. In her arms was a small black cat, its golden eyes wide and frightened, its long tail whipping back and forth.

"Whew!" Nora said in relief. "I was afraid our rat joke was turning out to be true."

"Isn't it beautiful?" Jennifer said, stroking the cat's back, trying to calm it down.

"And black, too," Susan commented. "The perfect color for a haunted house."

Obviously not liking the spotlight or the strangers, the cat suddenly twisted itself out of Jennifer's arms and landed lightly on the floor at her feet. Brushing by Nora again, it stopped at the head of the basement stairs, looked back over its shoulder and meowed, and then started down.

"It's inviting us to the witch's den," Nora joked, keeping her light on the cat as it padded silently down the stairs. When it reached the bottom, it turned a corner and disappeared into the inky darkness. "Okay," she said to the others, "here we go."

Slowly and carefully, the group made its way down the stairs. At the bottom, they found themselves in a large open space with crumbling brick walls and dark corridors branching off to the left and right. The place had a damp, musty smell, and the cement floor was gritty under their feet. Cobwebs draped the corners and hung from the ceilings like pieces of old, torn lace.

"I guess we're not going to find a rec room and a Ping-Pong table," Steve quipped, aiming his light down one of the narrow, low-ceilinged passageways. "Which way's the dining room?"

"Back upstairs," Mia said immediately, pulling off a cobweb that had attached itself to one of her spikes. "But I know that's not what you meant." She glanced back at the stairs and then up at the ceiling. "The dining room's over that way," she said, pointing to the passageway on the left.

"That's right," Nora said in surprise, having just figured it out herself. "You have a good sense of direction, Mia."

"That'll come in handy," Jason commented. "She can be our navigator if we get lost."

"I'm not afraid of getting lost," Lucy said, shivering from the dampness. "But I really hate the idea of freezing to death. Why don't we get moving?"

"Good idea." Tommy pointed to Nora and grinned. "Lead on, Macduff!"

Forming themselves into a line again, the group set off down the passageway, which twisted and snaked and took so many turns that not even Mia could tell what part of the house they were under. The batteries in two of the flashlights died, but Jennifer assured Nora that they could still see her. "I told you that yellow sweater would come in handy," she teased.

But Nora didn't answer. The passageway had come to an end, and up ahead, in the beam of her flashlight, she could see a wooden door set into the wall. Sitting at the foot of the door, staring back at her, was the black cat.

"Well," Nora whispered, as the others bunched up behind her, "who wants to open the door?"

As if in answer, the cat stood up, arched its back in a stretch, then tapped its paw against the door, which swung open slightly on silent, well-oiled hinges.

There was no need to use their flashlights; there was light coming from the room, and as the cat pushed its way inside, widening the opening, they could see a dim lamp shining on a rickety wooden box.

Before anyone could move, a shadow — definitely a human shadow — wavered across the doorway, and a man's voice from inside the room said, "So, I've been discovered, have I? Well, whoever you are, I congratulate you!"

Five minutes later, after the two teachers had spoken to the man, everyone except Mia and Ms. Spencer (who then went to get Miss Mandeville), stepped nervously inside the room. It was as damp and crumbling as the rest of the basement, but it did have a few things to make it comfortable — two old lamps, a piece of rug thrown over the cement floor, an electric coffeepot, a couple of battered tables, and two sagging easy chairs.

There were other things in the room, too: cables and wires snaking across the ceiling and walls, and on a table by one of the easy chairs was what looked like a complicated control box, with buttons and knobs and sliding levers.

The man who had invited them inside stood silently in the center of the floor, holding the cat, and watched as Andy studied the control box. After a minute, Andy reached out a finger and pushed one of the buttons. Tinny, old-fashioned music came out of the microcassette they'd taken from the second floor hallway.

The man smiled ruefully, "Congratulations again," he said.

Nora pointed at the box. "I'll bet those other buttons control magnets, don't they? Magnets in the ceiling and the walls that make certain pieces of furniture move around?"

"Very good," the man said. He chuckled.

"I don't see what's so good about it," Tracy whispered to Jennifer. "Or so funny, either."

But Jennifer was looking at the man and didn't answer. He had round pink cheeks, sparkling blue eyes, and a clear voice. He looked vaguely familiar. No, he looked *very* familiar.

"You," she said, "You're. . . ."

"James!" Miss Mandeville cried, coming into the room with Mia and Ms. Spencer.

"Exactly!" Jennifer said.

"Her brother?!" Tracy squeaked. "I thought he was in Europe."

Miss Mandeville obviously thought so, too. "Jimmy, what on earth are you doing here?" she demanded.

"It's a long story, Judy," he said, not sounding amused anymore.

She looked around the cold, dingy room. "Well," she said finally, seeming to recover from her shock, "if it's long, then I suggest we go upstairs to hear it. It's dark up there, too, but at least it's warmer."

"And the furniture won't move around," Jason added, as they all started to leave.

"It better not," Tracy said. "One ghost is enough. For a lifetime!"

Back in the dining room, everyone listened in unbroken silence as James Mandeville told his story. They'd relit the candles and started a fire in the fireplace, so the room was once more cozy and as bright as it could be without electricity. But the light and the coziness couldn't get rid of the strangeness of the story he told.

He had gone to Europe, as Miss Mandeville said. But he hadn't stayed. Furious that he'd been cut out of the will, he was determined to get Mandeville Manor back for himself. Once he heard that his sister had turned it into a lodging house, he realized that if he could make the business fail, she'd probably sell, and then he could step in.

He was an inventor, he reminded his sister,

and after several secret, nighttime visits (after all, he knew this place as well as anyone, having grown up here) he had all the mechanics in place, and the control room set up in the basement, which no one had used in years.

He didn't live in the basement, of course; he lived a few miles away and did his shopping in Rockford, so no one in Piedmont would see him. But he frequently walked the grounds of Mandeville Manor, unnoticed by anyone, so he knew when there were guests. And it was the easiest thing in the world to slip into the house, down to the basement, and set things in motion, as he put it.

"To tell you the truth," he said, stroking the cat which was curled up in his lap, and which, he said, had been his only companion for five years, "this was going to be my last performance, so to speak, even if I hadn't been discovered."

"Why?" Jennifer asked. "Because you knew how badly Mandeville Manor was doing?"

James shook his head. "No. Oddly enough, as time went by, I stopped feeling so angry." He thought a minute and then said, "Or maybe it isn't so odd. All I really wanted was to be a part of Mandeville Manor again, but the method I chose was hurting my sister. And she wasn't to blame for anything."

"I certainly wasn't!" Miss Mandeville said indignantly. "Good heavens, Jimmy, if you hadn't run off to Europe so fast, I would have told you that you were welcome to stay here."

"You would?"

"Of course! Do you think I ever cared whether you were a banker or not?" She shook her head and laughed. "After what you've done here with all your gadgets, I'm convinced you found the right calling!"

"That's for sure," Mitch remarked quietly to Tommy. "He could probably get a patent on the stuff he set up in this house."

"In fact, you can start living here now," Miss Mandeville went on, "although I have no idea how much longer we can afford to keep it."

"Maybe it's not too late," Jennifer suggested. "I mean, you could keep on running it together. And we could spread the word about it, like Mitch said before."

"And this time, it would be the truth," Nora said.

"I'd like nothing better than that," Mr. Mandeville said hopefully. "I think I might be a big help. After all, I'm very handy."

Miss Mandeville laughed again. "It's certainly worth a try," she said.

"Isn't this great!" Tracy said. "I love happy endings."

"Speaking of endings," Mr. Rochester commented, stifling a yawn, "it's three-thirty in the morning. What do you say we all get to bed and let the Mandevilles catch up on the last five years?"

Suddenly, everyone was yawning. The excitement was over, and the lack of sleep had finally caught up with them. They said goodnight to the Mandevilles, who were already discussing plans for keeping the house, and filed out into the hallway.

"After this," Denise said, her eyes drooping with tiredness, "*Macbeth* isn't going to seem very dramatic at all."

"Nothing's going to seem dramatic after this," Lucy agreed. "What a plot! Shakespeare would have loved it."

Mia yawned widely as they started upstairs. "Do you think we'll ever go on a field trip where nothing happens?"

"A normal field trip?" Nora laughed. "I hope not. We'd get too bored."

They were getting close to the second floor when Jennifer nudged Nora. "Look!" she whispered excitedly.

"Not more ghosts," Susan groaned, hearing her. "I couldn't stand it."

"No, not ghosts," Jennifer whispered. "Just look, up at the top of the stairs!"

Everyone looked. The two teachers had just reached the head of the stairs and, to everyone's satisfaction, they were holding hands once again.

"Another happy ending," Tracy sighed.

"Operation Lovesave," Jennifer giggled, "was a resounding success."

In another minute, everyone was gathered in the second floor hallway. "We'll have to get up early to straighten up the remains of our search," Mr. Rochester told them, looking at the dismantled light fixture in the ceiling. "But you can get a little extra sleep on the bus into Rockford." He smiled, still holding Ms. Spencer's hand. "You did good work tonight," he said. "Oh, by the way, something else happened that I thought you might be able to explain."

They all looked at him curiously. He reached into a pocket and pulled out a folded piece of paper. "I found this on the floor in my room earlier," he said.

No one said a word.

"I got one, too," Ms. Spencer grinned, holding up a similar piece of notepaper.

Silence.

"I think whoever delivered them got confused," Mr. Rochester said, "because mine starts out, 'Dear Allison.' "

"And mine begins with 'Dear Cliff,'" Ms. Spencer told them.

I got the notes mixed up, Tracy thought in horror. She would have confessed right on the spot, except that Nora and Jennifer both poked her in the back.

"Since you've proven yourselves so good at solving mysteries," Mr. Rochester said, his dark eyes sparkling, "we were hoping you could solve just one more."

Everyone studied the floor for a minute, trying to think up a good story. Finally, Jennifer looked up.

"Gosh," she said so innocently that the drama teacher would have been proud, "I just can't think of a thing." She glanced at Nora, who was trying to keep a straight face. "I guess you'll just have to blame it on The Ghost of Mandeville Manor!"

Nora, Jen, and Lucy have just overheard a very strange conversation. Is someone planning a bank robbery in Cedar Groves? Read Junior High #14, JUNIOR HIGH PRIVATE EYES.